T3-BOA-895

PRAISE FOR AURORA ROSE REYNOLDS

"No other author can bring alpha perfection to each page as phenomenally as Aurora Rose Reynolds can. She's the queen of alphas!"

~Author CC Monroe

"Aurora Rose Reynolds makes you wish book boyfriends weren't just between the pages."

~Jenika Snow *USA Today* Bestselling Author

"Aurora Rose Reynolds writes stories that you lose yourself in. Every single one is literary gold."

~Jordan Marie *USA Today* Bestselling Author

"No one does the BOOM like Aurora Rose Reynolds"

~Author Brynne Asher

"With her yummy alphas and amazing heroines, Aurora Rose Reynolds never fails to bring the BOOM."

~Author Layla Frost

"Aurora Rose Reynolds alphas are what woman dream about."

~Author S. Van Horne

"When Aurora Rose Reynolds lowers the BOOM, there isn't a reader alive that can resist diving headfirst into the explosion she creates."

~Author Sarah O'Rourke

"Aurora Rose Reynolds was my introduction into Alpha men and I haven't looked back!"

~Author KL Donn

OTHER BOOKS BY AURORA ROSE REYNOLDS

The Until Series

Until November

Until Trevor

Until Lilly

Until Nico

Second Chance Holiday

Underground Kings Series

Assumption

Obligation

Distraction

Infatuation

Until Her Series

Until July

Until June

Until Ashlyn

Until Harmony

Until December

Until Him Series

Until Jax

Until Sage

Until Cobi

Shooting Stars Series

Fighting to Breathe

Wide-Open Spaces

One Last Wish

Fluke my life series

Running into love

Stumbling into love

Tossed into love

Drawn Into Love

Ruby Falls

Falling Fast

Alpha Law CA ROSE

Justified

Liability

Finders Keepers

One More Time (Coming soon)

How To Catch An Alpha

Catching Him

Baiting Him

Hooking Him

To Have To Hold To Keep

Trapping Her

Taking Her (Coming Soon)

Stalking Her (Coming Soon)

OTHER BOOKS BY JESSICA MARIN

Let Me In Series

Heartbreak Warfare

Perfectly Lonely

Edge of Desire

Bear Creek Rodeo Series

The Irish Cowboy

The Celtic Cowboy

For You Series (Hockey Romance)

Yearn For You (Coming Soon)

Stand Alone Novels

Until Valerie

(Part of Aurora Rose Reynolds' Happily Ever Alpha World)

One

"*Y*OU'RE LISTENING TO 103.6 *BOOM!* Country Nashville, and that was Gavin McNeer's new single, 'User'. Speaking of the new heartthrob of country music, he's our special guest in the studio this morning. What's up, Gavin?" The radio disc jockey, Trevor Ant, nods at me while pressing some buttons on his audio console, signaling for my turn to speak into the microphone.

"Good morning, everyone," I say, unable to hide my southern drawl or the deep, husky tone of my voice. "Thanks for letting me crash your morning routine." I turn around in surprise hearing muffled screams coming from behind me. A crowd of women have gathered on the other side of the glass, watching our interview. I see my cousin and full-time assistant, Sosie, rolling her eyes at the squealing from the ladies when I point and wave to them. I chuckle at Sosie, her disdain for my overexuberant female fans always amusing me.

"Please excuse the background noise, as Gavin has accumulated a large crowd in the hallway," Trevor reports to the listeners, irritation radiating in his eyes at the unwelcome visitors. Trevor Ant is a veteran radio disc jockey, having a long tenure on one of Nashville's most popular country radio stations. He runs a tight ship and likes his routine to be smooth and uninterrupted. And I'm sure having a gaggle of women outside is not part of his plan for this interview.

"Where did they even come from? They were not there five minutes ago," I wonder out loud as I turn around again and give them a thumbs-up, causing another round of high-pitched hysterics to bellow into the room. I laugh at Sosie again, enjoying getting another rise out of my sassy cousin.

"The real question, Gavin, is where did you come from, and more importantly, where have you been all my life?" CeeCee Walker purrs, licking her lips in a way that is purely intentional for me to see. CeeCee is Trevor's female sidekick, reporting mostly on the gossip in the music industry. While Trevor has an exceptional reputation, word on the street is that CeeCee has no remorse trading air play for a roll in the sheets when she sets her sights on a musician she's interested in. Even worse is that she's supposed to be "happily" married.

"I was born and raised in Austin, Texas and have been living in Nashville for four years now," I answer, not even acknowledging her last comment. My insides burn with annoyance. I might be forced to be cordial and polite, but it pisses me off when women play games. And there is no way in hell I'd ever give her any reason to think I'm interested in her advances.

Mental Note: Stay very far away from CeeCee Walker.

"So, Texas is where that sexy drawl comes from. I must report to the ladies listening that Gavin looks just as good as he sounds! Like a tall glass of sweet tea on a hot summer's day."

I smile coldly at her while shifting uncomfortably in my seat. I'm fortunate to be the son of two very good-looking parents, but talking about my looks is always my least favorite subject. I take care of myself by working out daily, and I know how blessed I am to be talented and handsome, but sometimes being both is a double-edged sword.

Don't get me wrong—I'm not complaining about it. It just makes me have to work that much harder at my craft. I'm not always taken seriously and have been accused more than once that my voice is autotuned in the studio and that the only reason I've been this successful is because of my looks. People who've worked with me know that isn't true, but some assholes like to say otherwise.

I give zero fucks about what is reported about me by the media, and I won't even acknowledge those lowlifes who just want to ride on my coattails. I'm more than happy to prove them wrong by inviting them into the studio with me. Looks fade, but my music is going to last a lifetime, and that's all I care about.

4

The haters can go fuck themselves.

"While you might be new to us as a singer, you're no stranger to the music business. You've actually been writing and producing songs for other artists for a while now. Tell us how you broke into the industry, Gavin, as it's not an easy task," Trevor interjects, giving CeeCee a look that is screaming at her to behave.

"That's right, Trevor. It sure isn't an easy industry to get into, much less recognized. For the one song that makes it, thousands of others will never see the light of day. A lot of this business is who you know and timing. My brother and I had our own band back in Austin, where we got discovered—"

"Oh my gosh, there's another one of you?" CeeCee screeches out in excitement, causing Trevor to throw his hands up in exasperation. I again choose to ignore her and focus my attention on answering his question.

"Unfortunately, nothing came to fruition from our former record deal, but one of our songs was discovered by an artist, who asked us to come to Nashville to help them record it. My brother had some personal issues that forced him to stay back in Austin, so I came out here by myself and just got lucky meeting the right people at the right time. I've proven myself as a songwriter and have been fortunate to experience success with some talented artists."

"One of those songs sat at the number one spot on the country radio charts for weeks. Congratulations on that! What was it like writing 'Thief of Your Heart' with Tori Langston?" I nod at Trevor's question and plaster a smile on my face, trying to hide my aggravation at his mentioning my ex-girlfriend. His question is legitimate, and it's only natural that he would ask. After all, that hit song I wrote for her did help take my career to the next level and has been playing non-stop on the radio.

"Thanks, Trevor. It's very exciting and humbling to have had that song at number one and now have 'User' in the number two spot on the charts. Tori was great, her voice perfect for the vision of the song." I keep my answer brief, hoping they move the conversation on to a different subject, because Tori Langston is the last person I want to continue talking about.

"Rumor has it, Gavin, that you wrote 'User' in response to Tori breaking up with you. Can you tell us if she really was the inspiration behind it?" CeeCee smiles snidely, knowing full well that my publicist told them no personal questions about my former relationship with Tori. Clearly, she doesn't give two shits what they told her and is hoping that putting me publicly on the spot like this will warrant her the answer she's craving to hear. I don't care if CeeCee Walker can help my career with airplay; I will never talk about my private life, nor would I ever badmouth my ex.

Even though our break-up was kept quiet, everyone in the industry knows this song is about her. If people followed the timeline of our relationship to our break-up and then the release of the song, it's a no-brainer. But my private life has always been a do-not-even-go-there subject, and I refuse to capitalize off even mentioning her name. What makes it worse is that Tori's father is the owner of the label who signed me. The same label Tori is signed with.

Avoiding her question, I lean into the mic

before me. "I think everyone can relate to the lyrics, whether they've been used by a friend, family member, co-worker, or even a lover. It's their own interpretation of that specific relationship and how it made them feel that causes the song to speak to them. We've all been used for something before, haven't we, CeeCee?" I give her a cheeky wink, my eyes daring her to continue questioning me. I can play this mind fuck game all day long if I have to and will thoroughly enjoy it. CeeCee Walker thinks I need her, but she has no idea who she's dealing with.

While the asshole part of me was hoping she would continue, I'm happy to see the look of resignation settle into her eyes and her lips tighten in disappointment. "Yes, we most certainly all have," she responds back. "Now that you're signed with Charisma Records, will you be hitting the road?"

"Eventually, yes. I would love to start with some of the bigger summer festivals and then hit the smaller venues during the fall. For now, we have one more single to release before the album comes out."

"I think I speak for me and everyone else

when I say we are looking forward to hearing the rest of the album, Gavin. Thank you so much for stopping by this morning. Let's send you off by playing another song you wrote. This is 'My Town' by Scotty Wilkins."

I hold my breath, waiting for the lights of the **On Air** sign to go off, and once they do, I immediately take off my headphones and stand up, ready for this interview to be over with. Before I can even say thank you, the door swiftly opens and an intern comes in, asking if I can take a photo with Trevor and CeeCee for their social media pages. I oblige and turn toward Trevor once the picture is snapped and thank him for having me on his show. I slowly start inching my way to the door while saying my goodbyes, hoping to get out of here as quickly as I possibly can without coming across as being rude.

CeeCee Walker dashes those hopes by blocking the door, forcing me to stop and talk to her.

"It was so nice meeting you today, Gavin." Her eyes take their sweet ol' time traveling up and down my body as if I'm a piece of meat she's picking out at the butcher's shop.

"I already volunteered myself to cover your record release party. Here's my card; think of me if you ever want someone to accompany you to some of these industry events." She hands me her card and catches me off guard by planting a kiss dangerously close to the side of my lips.

"Thanks, but I already have my plus-one covered," I politely tell her with a small smile and a curt nod. Suddenly, a large banging noise comes from the glass, startling CeeCee and moving her attention away from me.

"We've got to go. Get out of his way!" Sosie yells at her through the glass, and I have to bite my lower lip to keep from laughing.

Fuck, now I gotta give Sosie a bonus for being her bitchy self today.

"Thanks again!" I dip my chin at CeeCee and slip out of the room into the crowded hallway. Shit, so much for getting out of here quickly, I think as a crowd of ladies circles around me. My fans are the reason my songs are sitting pretty on the charts, so even though I want to take off, I make time for them by signing autographs and taking photos before finally heading to our car.

"Please tell me the rest of the interviews we have lined up for today aren't going to be as torturous as that one?" I sigh as soon as the doors to the car are closed.

"CeeCee Walker is the only barracuda on the agenda for today," Rachel, my A&R rep from the label, informs me and Sosie with a smirk, causing us to laugh at her accurate description of CeeCee. "The rest of today should be smooth sailing."

"Thanks for saving me back there, Sos." I ruffle the top of her hair like I used to do when we were kids, prompting her to slap my hand away while giving me a dirty look. She pinches my bicep hard in retaliation before rummaging through her purse for a brush to fix her hair.

With a deep breath, I remind myself that this is *my* time right now. I've hustled and worked hard to be in the position I'm now in, and I'll enjoy every damn minute of it. No one is going to ruin this opportunity for me. I clap my hands and rub them together, refusing to let a leech like CeeCee Walker put me in a bad mood. "Let's have fun and get this show on the road!" I exclaim as the car drives us to our next interview.

Two

ALY

I VAGUELY HEAR the mumbling sound of what appears to be someone's voice as I slowly start to wake up. The soothing voice starts off in almost a whisper, but gains volume, recognition starting to alert my senses. The low, smooth male voice proceeds to get louder and louder until it reaches a crescendo into the opening chorus. I smile as Bono from U2 tells me it's a beautiful day and I shouldn't let it get away.

You're right, Bono! I won't!

Every morning, I choose to wake up to this song—one of my all-time favorites—hoping it sets the tone for my day to be beautiful, to be exciting. *To be memorable.*

My smile widens as I open my eyes to see the sunlight creeping in through my curtains, telling me it's going to be another gorgeous day here in Nashville. I throw the covers off me, put my slippers on, and start my morning routine of getting ready for work. After I take care of business in the bathroom and shower, I head to the kitchen to make coffee.

While the coffee brews, I fill my cat's bowl up with his breakfast before making my own. I pour myself a bowl of cereal, grab my cup of joe, and sit down to start eating. As usual, I stare off into space while my mind thinks of all the things I need to accomplish today. Apollo jumping on the table startles me out of my trance, and even though I should yell at him to get down, I instead scratch behind his fluffy ears where his sweet spot is.

"We're going to rock this day, aren't we, Apollo?"

Yup, I'm *that* girl. That girl who's the optimist, the romanticist with a bohemian, hippie flair and Goody Two-shoes way of life. I'm that girl who thinks the glass is always half full and am grateful for every day I get to wake up and live another day. One might call my exuberance for life annoying, but in a world where life can become dark and depressing in the blink of an eye, I call my positivity "survival." My happiness and love for life makes people roll their eyes, but honestly, I'm beyond the point where I care what other people think. If they want to live their life with doubt, stress, and anxiety, then so be it. I choose to be this way, and let me make it perfectly clear, I'm damn happy to be *that* girl.

When I'm done eating breakfast, I load the dirty dishes into the dishwasher before heading back to my room to brush my teeth and finish getting ready for work. Once my hair is done and makeup is complete, I grab my purse and car keys and head out the door. The beautiful morning sky makes me wish I could walk to work, but because my hours are unpredictable, it's safer for me to drive, even if I only live a couple miles away. I live in the same house my parents did when they went to college - a rental property my grandparents bought as an investment located between where Belmont and Vanderbilt Universities are.

When my parents took it over, they completely gutted and updated it with modern fixtures with the intention of selling it to make some money. Because of the exclusive area it was in, they decided to keep it instead of selling it. My sister, Valerie, and her best friend, Emma, lived in it during their college years, and then I moved in when it was my time to start college. I was hoping Valerie was going to continue living here when I moved in, but because she's four years older than me and needed quietness while she worked and studied to become a certified CPA and auditor, she decided to move into her own condo close by. My best friend, Willow, was living with me up until we graduated and then moved out to be closer to her new job.

I make the quick drive to my office and pull into the parking lot. I still can't believe I'm actually working in the music industry. I've always known I wanted some sort of career in the music world. Music has always spoken to my soul, starting out when I was a little girl and my mother would play classical music for me to fall asleep to. I studied piano and violin but grew more interested in the business and gossip side of the industry when I was in high school. Just driving up and down Music Row excited me, knowing how much history was behind those walls of the famous music houses.

I immersed myself into researching what I needed to do to start my path into the industry. I applied and got accepted into Belmont University and studied in their music business program. I busted my butt in school, knowing if I really wanted this, I was going to have to stand out amongst all the other students who had the same dream as I did. Fortunately, I found a cute, boutique-style record label called Big Little Music to intern at during my senior year. Nashville is known for country music, but all genres of music are produced and recorded here. Big Little Music started off with indie rock artists, but it now has a full catalog of music and represents some of the biggest names in the industry. Proving to my bosses I'm a hard, loyal worker paid off, and I was offered an assistant's position in the A&R department as soon as I graduated. It's been three months since graduation, and most of my college classmates still don't have a job, so I know how truly blessed I am.

There are a lot of perks that come with my job, from working with famous artists, to planning VIP parties, to attending concerts and award ceremonies. I take every single assignment I'm given seriously, because if I want to move up in this world, I have to act professionally, be on time, and never, *ever* act star-struck when in the presence of a celebrity, even if I am star-struck. The biggest rule of them all, one I set for myself is that I don't date men in the industry, especially good-looking musicians.

I walk in and wish a good morning to anyone whose path I cross on the way to my office. I sit down, turn on my computer, and start making my to-do list for the day. Every morning, I arrive one hour earlier than my boss in order to catch up on emails and relish in the silence, because once he arrives, my day—and sometimes my evening—is filled with chaos.

Fifty-four minutes later, I hear his booted footsteps coming and look up from my computer. "Good morning, Sunshine," Shane Adams sings in greeting before resuming his phone conversation and shutting his office door. Shane is one of the A&R managers here, and boy did I hit the boss lottery when he hired me. He acts more like my big brother and trusts me enough to let me do my job, gently guiding me along the way when he feels I need help. There are two other assistants who report to him, but they don't have the close relationship he and I share. I can't explain it, but we just clicked from day one. He makes every day at work an adventure and keeps things exciting for me and the rest of the people on staff.

Moments later, he comes right back out of his office with his empty coffee mug and parks his hip against my desk. "I'm going to get more caffeine and then let's get together for our morning meeting. We have lots to discuss, and I need to meet with all my staff before eleven thirty."

"Sounds good," I respond with a smile, but internally, I'm questioning how much we really have to discuss. *Is there something I'm forgetting?* I wonder, glancing at my short to-do list once Shane walks away from my desk. I shrug my shoulders in confusion, since I'm sure I will soon find out what else is going to be added to my plate. I grab my notebook and pen and wait for him to return to his office.

"All right," he drawls out once he shuts his door and walks around his desk to sit behind it. "Let's get down to business." He folds his hands together and stares at me intently. "Please tell me you've heard back from that hot hockey player and have a date lined up with him."

I burst out laughing at his eager expression while he waits for me to answer him. Only Shane would consider my love life as the most important topic of business to start off our morning meeting.

"Yes, he has called me. But!" I hold up my hand to stop him from screaming with glee. "I'm honestly only interested in being his friend." Ever since my college boyfriend dumped me a year ago, men have been the last thing I'm interested in. I'm just starting to figure out what I want to do with my life and what I need to do to reach my goals. And if I'm honest with myself, my busy work schedule doesn't leave me much time to date. Heck, I can barely give attention to my cat—much less a man!

"Alyson Dawson, what is wrong with you? Do you know how many women would die to have Brodie Larsen calling them?" He looks at me with such disdain that I start laughing again. Brodie Larsen is a hotshot NHL player who comes from a very famous hockey family. His father played for the Predators and Brodie was actually born here in Nashville. Fans went crazy when the Predators drafted him straight out of college, and he has been one of the more popular players since then.

Our marketing department decided it would be a good idea to give tickets to the local sports teams to any concerts our artists were having in hopes they would come and return the favor to us with hockey tickets. Brodie and two other players showed up to our suite at the arena during one of our clients' concerts. I knew of Brodie, but was surprised at how good-looking he was with his dark hair, intense blue eyes, and lean, hard body.

He was not shy at all in introducing himself to me, and I enjoyed chatting with him, but I didn't get the sense he was interested in me. Not that it mattered, because I definitely didn't feel any sparks for him, so imagine my surprise when he asked for my number at the end of the evening. I didn't hesitate in giving it to him, thinking it would be cool to have a potential new friend.

"Actually, I think I want to set him up with my best friend, Willow. She's drop-dead gorgeous and would be right up his alley." I tap my fingers together with an evil smile forming on my face. The more I think about the idea, the more I think Willow might be perfect for him. Now I just have to figure out how to get the two of them together.

"And what do you think you are, chopped liver? Why are you giving up on him so easily? You deserve some young, hot stud pampering you. Besides, you two would make really pretty babies."

I shake my head at Shane and his reference of babies. No way am I anywhere near ready for a husband and babies. I want to establish myself and get in some traveling before settling down. Maybe that's why guys are not even a priority on my to-do list right now.

"I know I'm a catch." I roll my eyes. "I just don't think Brodie is the one for me."

"How would you even know if you don't

give him a chance?" Shane questions with a knowing smile.

"It sounds to me like you're the one who wants to give him a chance. Why don't you go ask him out?" I counter, knowing full well that Shane Adams doesn't like to step away from a challenge when one is presented to him.

"Child please, only in my dreams would that man slap his stick for me."

I close my eyes to get rid of the mental image he just put in my brain. If our offices were bugged, human resources would be mortified at our conversations.

"I think this conversation has gone far enough. Shouldn't we talk about more pressing matters, like work?" I suggest, not wanting to discuss Brodie Larsen or my singlehood any longer.

"This conversation is called me being concerned about your work/life balance. So no, I am not ready to change the subject yet." He huffs, causing me to chuckle at his flair for drama. "Why do you act like a sixty-seven-year-old in a twenty-three-year-old body? All you do is go home and read books. You aren't going to meet a real-life man if you are holed up all night with your fictional ones. Those men you read about aren't real. Real men are flawed, whine, grow fat, and forget birthdays."

I raise an eyebrow at him, questioning if he's talking about his real-life experience from his ex-boyfriend.

"Look, all I'm saying, Aly, is I think you need to incorporate a little more fun in your life. Start expanding your circle outside your sister and friends. Date a little so you can find out what type of man you do want…when you're ready to meet 'the one'." He sighs as he looks over at me before putting on his reading glasses. "And with that, my dear, I am ready to change subjects and talk business."

"Thank goodness, because these last two minutes have been a snooze fest," I say sarcastically, causing Shane to narrow his eyes at me.

"Are we all set for the Bluebird Cafe tomorrow?" he asks in his formal business voice, indicating we really are done with the inquisition of my non-existent love life. Tomorrow is industry night at the famous Bluebird Cafe, and we have lined up a mixture of existing successful musicians with some up-and-coming singers.

"Yes, all talent have been told their times to report and everyone has turned in their song lists." I slide the sheet of paper over to Shane, who nods his approval.

"Did you tell Scotty Wilkins that if his cute ass doesn't show up on time, I'm taking everything off his rider?" Shane asks in exasperation at the mere mention of our most difficult artist. We signed Scotty Wilkins off of one of those reality singing shows, thinking the man who was on television was going to be easy, accommodating, and appreciative of the opportunities thrown his way.

We were dead wrong - Scotty Wilkins is one of our most difficult clients. And since he's one of our more famous clients, he usually gets his way every time.

"Those weren't my exact words to him, but I did tell him a call time that was an hour earlier than everyone else's."

"That's my girl." Shane nods in approval once more. "Did we receive a list of artists Charisma Records is showcasing?"

"No, and I have called and emailed over there asking for their artists' names and song lists multiple times. Remind me again why we invited them to participate in an event we are supposed to be hosting?" It's a lot of work having to rally up our own talent, but adding another label's talent to the mix has turned it into a nightmare.

"We technically didn't invite them. Big Daddy Langston heard how successful it was becoming and wanted to get Charisma into the mix. I have zero doubts he offered up a pretty penny to the Bluebird owners for a permanent spot on Tuesdays. You know he runs this town." I've seen Atticus Langston from afar at many events but haven't met him personally. Not only does he own Charisma Records, but also multiple investments and properties around Nashville. He's called "Mr. 615" for a reason - and that's because his money has helped build this city up and put it on the map with the help of producing a hit television show that skyrocketed our population.

A knock on the door interrupts us and one of the interns pops his head in. "Mrs. Davidson would like to see you, sir." He locks eyes with Shane.

Kathleen Davidson is a force to be reckoned

with in the industry. She started this label fifteen years ago when she was a struggling artist not being treated the way she felt she should've been. She worked two extra jobs to save the money to start up the label herself. Then with some heavy scouting, taking her around the country, she found her first successful artist and since then has had continuous success and fame. Her artists like her hands-on approach, so she keeps her staff small, making sure we cultivate and maintain close relationships with each artist. Her strategy of maintaining a label with the southern hospitality feel to it has worked so far and even has her competing for talent with the big guns like Charisma.

"Kathleen can help us get a list of Charisma's artists for tomorrow," Shane tells me while jotting down a quick note on the pad he's writing on. "Let me go talk to her now and ask her for help. In the meantime, I need you to call the Predators and make sure we have a suite for next week's game against Detroit. Order food and beverages and then start up the guest list of artists we think need to make an appearance." I add that to my to-do list and follow him out of his office.

The wheels in my head start turning, as this might be the perfect opportunity to introduce Willow to Brodie. I write down a reminder to ask Shane if I can bring a plus-one, knowing full well he will say yes. I smile to myself, ready to take on the matchmaker roll for my best friend, who won't even see it coming.

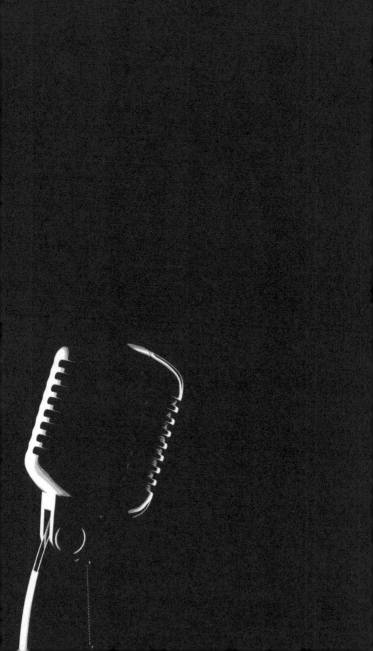

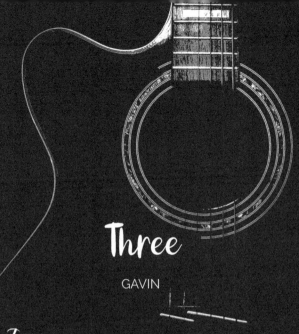

Three

GAVIN

I DRUM MY fingers against the car door panel, impatient energy coursing through my veins while watching the outside scenery pass by. Sosie is driving us to my show tonight, and for some reason, I feel nervous. My pre-show jitters are usually due to the anticipation of the high I get while performing, so this nervousness is a foreign feeling. Maybe it's because I'm tired. Yesterday was a long day with continued interviews and time spent in the studio working on a song for another artist. I didn't get home until close to midnight and crashed as soon as I turned the lights off.

"What's up with you?" Sosie asks, giving me a strange look out of the corner of her eye. She notices everything, so I know I won't be able to weasel my way out of this unwanted conversation.

"Nothing. What's up with you and those bags under your eyes?" I question with concern as I study her more closely. She has her hair up in a messy bun and her thick red glasses on, but those glasses only accentuate the deep purple bags underneath her blue eyes. Something is going on with her that she's not sharing. When I'm in the studio working for other artists, Sosie isn't on the clock, meaning she was done working for me yesterday after lunch. What she does with her free time is her business, but when I see her not looking well, I make it a point to make her personal time my business.

"Always deflecting, but it won't work this time, Gav. I'm not answering your question until you answer mine." She gives me a sweet, fake smile before turning her attention back to the road.

"Fine," I mumble, caring more about hearing what's going on with her than my own nervousness. "Honestly, I don't know what the fuck is wrong with me. For some reason, I'm nervous."

"Yeah, I can tell. You're like the Tasmanian Devil over there." I follow her eyes to my left leg bouncing rapidly up and down. I place my hand on my thigh, mentally forcing it to stop. "But you've performed numerous times at the Bluebird. Why would this time be any different?"

"Possibly because this is a private event being held by another record label." *Their people will be watching me… judging me,* I think but don't say out loud. I shouldn't be nervous. I practically lived at the Bluebird Cafe when I first landed in Nashville. It's the place to play when you're a songwriter wanting to get noticed. It's an extremely small venue, capacity of only 90 people, making the audience seem like they're right on top of you. Food and beverages are served while the crowd listens to singers belt out their songs. The Bluebird has launched the careers of some of today's most famous singers like Taylor Swift and Garth Brooks. You can feel how special the place is the moment you walk through the doors.

"People are watching and judging you every time you walk on stage though," she reminds me.

"True." I sigh, not really wanting to psychoanalyze my mood right now.

"Maybe subconsciously, you're anxious because you know when your contract is up with the devil, you need to change record labels, and Big Little Music could potentially be your future home." I chuckle at her calling Atticus Langston the devil. From day one, Sosie saw right through his weaselly charm and loves telling me, in her heavily laced sarcastic voice that she prays for my soul every day.

"I don't think so. For one thing, I like being with a big label, because they have more dollars for marketing and advertising."

"That actually isn't true anymore," she informs me quietly. "I know you've heard how Big Little Music's artists love being with them. Plus, they've landed some pretty big names for not being a more well-known label." She starts rattling off the names of their well-known singers, surprising me with not only their lineup of talent, but her knowledge of who they have signed. When Sosie first started working for me, she didn't know shit about this industry. Not that it mattered to me—I was just trying to get her the fuck out of California and away from my toxic aunt and uncle. Since working for me, she has taken her job as my assistant very seriously, immersing herself in the industry, studying the ins and outs of it and who the big players are.

As I let her words settle in, I realize she might have a point. For a small label, Big Little Music has created quite the reputation for themselves. For one, they still care about their artists and not how much money they can get out of them. They are the total opposite of Charisma Records.

Up-and-coming artists like myself don't usually get signed by labels like Charisma. They already make enough money on their current catalog of talent and don't need or want to take a chance on nobodies. The only reason I got signed is because I wrote a hit song for Tori, who ran home and told her daddy about me. I highly doubt she raved about how truly talented I was—more like she wanted to keep me around and happy so I could write more songs for her. Fortunately, I signed only a single album deal with Charisma. Yes, it sucks big giant, Texas-sized balls that they get to own the rights to my songs for ten years, but that's the price you pay when you sign on the dotted line sometimes.

We pull into the parking lot behind the Bluebird. Since there are no dressing rooms for artists to wait in, most just arrive at their designated time slot or hang out with other performers in the back by their cars. I wave at a couple people I recognize as I get out of the car then retrieve my Martin D28 acoustic guitar from the back and start to warm up while standing there. Sosie always makes sure we arrive ten minutes before call time, which I know is padded with a few extra minutes. Once I'm warmed up, I head over to a group of people gathered near the back door.

"How's the crowd tonight?" I ask, greeting Scotty Wilkins with a pat to his shoulder. I've known Scotty for years and have even wrote a couple songs with him. Despite his overinflated ego, he's a good guy.

"Great crowd tonight. I might stick around

to make myself available, if you know what I mean." He winks at Sosie, who responds by rolling her eyes in disgust at him.

"You're barking up the wrong tree, man. My cousin would chew you up and spit you out." I give him a cold smile, hoping he catches my warning when our eyes lock. I know Sosie can handle herself, but I can't help the protectiveness I feel when it comes to my baby cousin. Anyone disrespects her, they'll answer to me.

Scotty chuckles and shakes his head while smiling. "You know, it's pretty awesome how tight you two are. I wish I had that family dynamic." For a moment, something that resembles sadness flashes in his eyes, but Scotty is quick to blink it away and go back to his usual cocky self.

What was that all about? Not that he would tell me anyway. We aren't close, nor will we probably ever be. I purposely keep my circle close and tight. In this industry, I've learned you don't know what people's motives are, so it's best to keep everyone at a distance until they prove themselves to be loyal.

"A couple of us are getting together next

week to jam. Look at your schedule, and if you're free, come join us. It would be worth your time." Having worked together before, Scotty knows how I operate. For him to say it would be worth my time piques my interest. I look over at Sosie, who nods at me while typing notes in her phone to check my schedule.

"I'll text you tomorrow with my schedule and you let me know where and when," I tell him, trying to remember what's going on next week. If I recall correctly, it's a slower week, with the end of the month being crazier.

"Good luck in there tonight," Scotty says with a nod at me. He pats me on the shoulder, waves at Sosie, and heads toward his car to leave.

"So much for him staying to make himself available," Sosie snarks sarcastically while watching him drive away.

"You like Scotty Wilkins?" I narrow my eyes at her, trying to gauge her reaction to my question. Sosie has shown zero interest in anyone since moving to Nashville. Her douchebag of an ex-boyfriend did a number on her, so it isn't that surprising to me that she's so standoffish when it comes to the opposite sex.

"Seriously, what *is* wrong with you tonight?" She huffs in annoyance, my smirk only seeming to rile her up even more. "That question doesn't even warrant a response. Get your head out of your ass, because it's time to perform." I laugh at her not-so-motivating pep talk and follow her up to the back door.

We check in with the staff and wait for them to signal me through. I hear the audience clapping and see the performer who was just on stage walk back to us. I smile in acknowledgment at her and then start walking when she's cleared the hallway. Once I appear into the main room, I keep a smile on my face, my eyes trained on the stool for me to sit on. The room is silent, no one applauding in greeting, because the rules of the Bluebird Cafe are that you are here to listen and immerse yourself in the experience and emotion of the songs. No one gets rowdy here. No one gets up to dance. This is a true, musical experience of listening and dissecting every word and meaning of these songs.

"Good evening, everyone. I'm Gavin." Introductions are always informal at the

Bluebird, because here, everyone is on equal ground. Doesn't matter how many accolades you have on your resume—we are all songwriters in this room, just trying to make a living doing what we love. My eyes scan the room, noting the heads nodding in recognition at me. I flash a genuine smile in their direction, forcing myself to hold it steady when noticing how many record label executives are here, some of them less than three feet away from me.

Calm the fuck down, Gavin, I tell myself after I talk about the background of the song I'm about to sing. I try to get into a comfortable position, placing my guitar on my thigh, take a deep breath, and close my eyes. I go through my meditation of zoning everyone out before internally repeating my personal motto:

You deserve to be here. Now show them why.

I peek down, watching my fingers strum the introductory notes to the very first song I wrote for someone else called "Needing You Now." My eyes slide closed once more when I start to sing, letting the familiar chords of the song wash away my nerves as I begin my tale.

I open them again so I can find that one focal point to concentrate on when I need it.

As I sing the last line of the first verse of the song, my eyes suddenly do a double take when they land on the face of one of the most beautiful women I've ever had the pleasure of looking at. Long, black lashes surround brown eyes the color of whiskey. Her face is lightly tanned with a dusting of natural-looking makeup brushed effortlessly across her face. Her hair seems to be the color of caramel, long and falling in waves down her shoulders. Her eyes are warm, inviting me into their abyss as everyone else starts to slowly fade away.

My mind screams at me not to blink, that she might be a figment of my imagination. As I start into the chorus, the emotions of the words force my eyelids shut, feeling the desperation of wanting that special someone to love you, support you, be there for you. I chose to sing this song tonight because of the power of its meaning and the emotions that it should evoke from the crowd.

My mind still pictures her as I sing out a long chord. My eyelids spring open, seeking out those stunning eyes as I mentally count the three beats of silence before continuing to the end of my narrative. I watch her expression as my voice registers up into my vibrato and an overwhelming need to impress her comes over me. Her eyes widen as I hit my note, her luscious pink lips parting in awe, telling me that I just nailed the ending of the song.

My heart beats rapidly in my chest as I stare at her while the crowd loudly cheers. I slowly start to smile at her, enjoying seeing her cheeks pinkening. She's sitting close enough that I can see the pupils in her eyes dilated from what I hope is pleasure. I reluctantly break our eye contact to acknowledge the crowd, thanking them before continuing to talk about the next song I plan on performing.

As I get ready to move on, I know right then and there she's going to be the one I sing to for the rest of my set, and I don't give a fuck if people start talking about how I'm staring at her like a creeper. I want to watch every single expression that crosses over that angelic face of hers. I start the chords to my next song, not even needing to look down, because the encouragement from her eyes is all I need. All I want.

This woman has captivated me like no one else has ever before.

I need to know the identity of the woman I can't take my eyes off of.

With our gazes locked together once more, I can't help but wonder who she is. Her attendance tonight means she's either in the industry or associated with someone in the industry. *Please, dear Lord, if she's associated with someone, let it not be a husband or a boyfriend.* The only other person at her table is another woman I don't know.

I look to see if I can spot a ring on her left hand when she takes a sip of whatever she's drinking. Her hand is bare, and I can't contain my smile knowing that the chances of her being married are slim without the hardware on. My only obstacle would be if there's a boyfriend, and it would be surprising if there wasn't. Most women who look like her are always taken, but then again, most women who are taken don't look at strangers the way she's looking at me.

She seems to be just as enthralled with me as I am with her. When I sing a seductive verse from my song, she rewards me with a sexy smirk that makes my dick instantly harden with want. I start to feel overheated and know damn well it isn't from the lights. This woman better be single, because my body is now buzzing with adrenaline, and a different kind of anticipation is now coursing through my veins.

I'm going to make that girl mine.

As soon as the song ends, I grab a bottle water and take a big gulp from it, my eyes never wavering from hers. I need to figure out a way to meet my mystery lady fast. I'm the last performer of the evening, and with this being an industry event, hours of socializing afterward usually occur. I have to talk to her before that happens and rapidly get her number, since we won't have any privacy once I'm done performing.

I'm about to sing my last song for my set and decide to change things up and sing the song I wrote for Tori, "Thief of My Heart." I see disappointment touch her eyes when I announce this will be my last song for the evening. Lord help me if this woman is as sweet and delectable as she looks, because if so, then I might just have to put myself out there.

Four

ALY

STOP STARING AT him, Aly!

He's going to think you are some pathetic psycho if you don't stop.

Wait, is he staring back at me?

Oh my God, he is!

I don't know what the hell is going on, but since the moment I locked eyes with Gavin McNeer, I haven't been able to look away. I've been staring at him for the last twenty minutes, infatuated with his voice, his eyes, his face…all of him. My body feels alive with a connective energy flowing between us, and with the way he's smiling back at me, he's either feeling it too or having pity on my poor, delusional soul.

You're crazy! my mind screams at my heart, and with the way my sister, Valerie, is looking at me when I glance in her direction, she's thinking the same thing.

I can't believe this is the first time I'm noticing him, *really* noticing him. It's not uncommon for songwriters to become performers, so Gavin hasn't really been on my radar the last two years. I've heard about his reputation as the gorgeous-as-sin songwriter from Austin who's extremely professional and talented. But any interest I had of learning more about the sexy Texan died when I saw the headlines that he was dating Tori Langston. This industry is small, and especially here in Nashville. We're all on pretty good terms, so everyone knows what a snake Tori can be.

When the gossip mill ran rampant about how and why they broke up, I didn't even bat an eyelash, because honestly, I wasn't surprised. I also couldn't care less. I have no desire to get caught up in the rumors, and sometimes, this industry gets a little incestuous with who dates who, which is another reason why I've stayed away from dating anyone in the business.

I take the opportunity to let my eyes wander while Gavin explains the next song he's about to sing. Pictures really don't do this man justice. They don't capture the sparkle in his green eyes when he looks at you or how his smile can be adorably crooked. You definitely can't appreciate from photos how well his clothes mold to his body. His short-sleeved T-shirt is white with a special low-cut V-neck that shows off his sternum, giving you a peak of a hard, muscled chest underneath. You can tell he's tall by how long his legs are, which are encased in dark denim that clings to his hard thighs and have stylish slits on his knees. His clothes might be plain, but I have no doubt they're probably designer labels.

I don't spend too much time assessing his body, because as soon as he starts singing again, my eyes are drawn right back to his handsome face. I become enraptured with his performance and start to daydream he's singing to me and only me.

"Why is he staring at you like that?" Valerie whispers in my ear while she nudges her elbow into my side once he finishes his song. "It's creeping me out!" I look at her and just blink my eyes, not understanding how she thinks he's creepy when all I see is how beautiful he is. She gives me a wide-eyed look and mouths, *What is wrong with you?*

I wish I had an answer for her, but for the life of me, I have no idea what's wrong with me. I've never reacted to someone this way before.

Snap out of it, Aly! He's just a man.

Yeah, a man who rattles my nerves by just looking at me. I turn my attention back toward him when he announces he will be performing his last song for the evening. I suddenly start to feel sad, as if this will be the last time I ever see him again, which is ridiculous, since we don't even know each other. He starts playing the first chords of "Thief of My Heart," and once again, his voice floods my senses and he weaves a dream around me with his lyrics.

You're the one for me.
I'm coming for you.
I'll steal your heart.
Run away with me.
Forever.

I keep my eyes locked on his as the song

becomes a tale of broken promises and hearts. Then, all too sudden, the song is over. I look around the room in a daze, seeing everyone on their feet, applauding. Then it dawns on me that every other woman is staring at him the same way I am. It's as if we've all been possessed by the devil himself. A devil we're all ready to sin with. Seeing their reactions snaps me out of my trance, and I start to wonder if I imagined how he was looking at me.

Don't be a fool, I tell myself, annoyed I let my mind wander for a man I've never even met before. I have zero clue as to what kind of person he even is. I give my head a shake and stand up to leave, telling myself that none of this matters anyway. He's a musician, and therefore, these silly fantasies of him will stay just that. *Fantasies.*

"Ready to go?" I ask Valerie, who's still looking at me with concern. She nods and we grab our purses off the back of our chairs to leave.

"Excuse me," I hear a husky voice say, making my head snap up to confirm who I hope it is. Gavin is standing in front of me, his height causing me to look up into his mesmerizing eyes. "Call me," he tells me in a commanding voice, handing me his card. My eyes widen in shock, causing his serious expression to change into a devastating smile. "Please?" There's a plea to his tone that turns my insides into complete mush. He's robbed me of my voice, so all I can do is smile back at him and nod. His gaze flashes briefly to my lips before looking back at me with apologetic eyes as people begin to approach us.

Soon, he's lost in the sea of bodies surrounding him, and I know our moment is gone. I clutch his card in my hand and turn to leave, shaking my head at my sister when she narrows her eyes at me and starts to open her mouth to ask questions.

"Not here," I interject with a stern voice before I turn away and search for the exit through the crowd. Just when we're about to clear the front door, I hear my name being called. I turn around to see Shane coming up behind me, motioning for me to meet him outside. With an unfamiliar pit in my stomach, I walk toward the end of the building to wait for Shane.

"Did I just witness Gavin McNeer giving you his card?" he inquires, staring me down with inquisitive eyes. Crap, if Shane saw that, then that means other people might've too.

"He sure did," Valerie answers for me, her gaze mirroring Shane's. Both of them cross their arms over their chests, and I know there's no way I'm getting out of this conversation right now.

"Do you know him? Because the way you two were eye-fucking each other all night long made even *me* feel uncomfortable."

I can't contain the blush that flushes up my cheeks from Shane's words. The evening air is cool, but just the mere thought of being in any kind of sexual position with Gavin is causing me to sweat.

"You're being dramatic." I wave my hand out in front of me, trying to downplay this situation, and the two of them just roll their eyes at me. "And no, I don't know him. Tonight was the first time I've ever seen him."

"And it looks like it won't be the last!" Shane breaks into an evil smile, rubbing his hands together as if he's coming up with a secret plan.

"He's a musician!" I sigh. "I'm sure he gives his card out to every single lady he thinks is pretty." I dismiss the two of them as I start to dig into my bag for my keys, not wanting them to make such a big deal out of something that probably doesn't mean anything.

"Actually, he doesn't," a voice comes up from behind us, startling me. I turn around to see a pretty blonde with a messy bun on top of her head and chic red glasses that match her lipstick standing next to us. She has startling baby-blue eyes that have a hint of annoyance to them. "Giving out his card to *anyone*," she says as she looks me over, "is something he doesn't do. In fact, I've never seen him give out his number to some random girl before. Regardless, I didn't mean to eavesdrop, but Gavin wanted me to remind you to call him later." She looks me up and down one more time before leaving without even introducing herself. Can we say *rude*?

"Wow, she's rude." Valerie huffs as we watch Gavin's messenger walk back inside the cafe. "Shane, do you know who she is?"

"I think that was his assistant, who's also his cousin. I always see her with him when it's work related. Who cares about her?" He groans. "Can we talk about how he sent her out here to remind you to call him not less than ten minutes after he gave you his number? That's hot!" Shane grips my forearm and squeezes, excitement radiating from his eyes. "You better do as he says and call him tonight."

"You know the policy, Shane," I remind him with a knowing smile. "No dating anyone in the industry."

"Rules are meant to be broken. Besides, that policy is for dating within our own company, not within the entire music industry!" He places his hands on his hips when I shake my head at him. "You listen to me, Alyson Marie Dawson…"

"Her middle name isn't Marie," Valerie tells him, and my lips twitch at seeing a *what the hell* expression on her face.

"I'm sure it isn't, but since I don't know what her middle name is and I'm trying to be all parental on her right now, Marie sounded good," he explains in exasperation, causing me to chuckle at how ridiculous he's being. "Listen to me, Alyson whatever-your-middle-name-is Dawson! You have got to stop letting these opportunities pass you by! First Brodie and now Gavin? Child, are you *insane?*" he screams the last word out.

"Can you lower your voice? You're causing a scene!" I hiss at him, not wanting the attention his shouting is bringing our way, judging by the looks we're starting to receive.

"All I'm saying is that you need to live a little and see where this goes. You may have just met your soul mate."

"Soul mate?" I scoff. Now it's my turn to roll my eyes at him.

He throws his arms up in irritation. "Valerie, can you please talk some sense into your sister?"

"Nope, I actually agree with her. I don't think she should call him. He's a musician, meaning girls throw themselves at him and he will also have to tour eventually. I don't approve of a long-distance relationship for my baby sister," Valerie states firmly, looking him in the eye to show how serious she is.

"Thanks for being supportive there, Val," Shane says with heavy sarcasm. "Side note— I'm really digging this hot-for-teacher look you've got going on with the sexy glasses and high ponytail. Too bad you're going to look this way when your ninety and single with that kind of attitude!"

Even Valerie can't contain her laughter at that comment. I do have to agree with Shane though on the subject of how my sister looks. She has a certain sex appeal in her work attire. She's gorgeous with her light-blonde hair and ice-blue eyes—the complete opposite of what I look like. Nobody guesses we're sisters when they first meet us, but our bond is as tight as if we were twins.

Shane looks between the two of us, shaking his head in silence. "I'm done with this conversation, as it's giving me heartburn and now I need a drink." He gives Valerie and me a kiss on our cheeks and looks one more time at us both. "It's a shame, really. Two of the most beautiful girls I've ever seen, single as the day they were born. Aly, I do hope you change your mind about calling Gavin. I'll see you tomorrow." And with that, he leaves us and goes back inside.

Valerie and I walk to our cars in silence, both of us deep in thought. Shane's words repeat over and over in my brain. What do I have to lose by calling Gavin? Sure, it goes against my policy of not dating musicians, but every cell in my body is screaming that he seems different and to give him a chance. The memory of his handsome face with those intense eyes demanding I call him causes me to shiver, a smile creeping up on my lips, because I actually liked that he demanded I call him.

Give him a chance, Aly! You've got nothing to lose.

Oh sure, just my heart if he breaks it into a million pieces.

A phone call is harmless and doesn't mean anything.

"You aren't seriously going to call him, are you?" Valerie's question interrupts my internal debate with myself. I look over at her to see she's waiting outside of her open car door, and I realize we didn't even say goodbye to each other, since I was lost in my own thoughts. I take a deep breath and flash her a bashful smile, knowing she isn't going to like my decision.

"Of course I am," I confirm, giving her a playful wink. Feeling high with adrenaline and confidence, I pull out my phone and type in his number. While his phone rings, I blow her a kiss goodbye and get into my car to start the engine. My Bluetooth picks up the call and I start to think I'll be leaving a voicemail when he suddenly picks up on the fourth ring.

"Hello?"

"Gavin? Um, hi, this is Alyson, the girl from the Bluebird Cafe," I say, trying to sound somewhat cute and not like a complete dork. "The one you gave your card to," I remind him, hoping he hasn't been handing his card out like candy on Halloween night.

"Alyson," he repeats my name in his deep voice, and a chill slides down my spine. "Do you go by Aly?"

"Yes," I rasp out, my voice shaking a little at my nervousness. "Most people call me Aly."

"Well, all right then… Aly." Why does my name sound so exotic coming from him? "I'm sorry if you can't hear me very well. I'm still at the Bluebird. Can I call you when I get home?"

"Oh right! I'm so sorry. Your assistant demanded I call you, and she's a little scary," I joke while I smack my hand against my head for being the dumbass I am. Of course he's still at the Bluebird, since it hasn't even been five minutes since I left. Why didn't I think to wait to call him?

Fortunately, he's chuckling at me and I marvel at the sound. "I hope she wasn't rude to you. Sosie's always pretty serious."

"No, she wasn't rude at all." I grimace at the lie. "Call me whenever you get a free moment. I should be up for a while. I mean, call me another day or whenever," I stammer, rolling my eyes at myself for how stupid I sound.

"I'll call you in a little bit, darlin'. Get home safe and I'll talk to you soon," he tells me before saying goodbye and hanging up.

"What an idiot you are, Aly," I groan out loud, mad at myself for calling him so soon and seeming desperate. Knowing there is nothing I can do about it now, I turn on the radio, hoping it will distract me from my thoughts of Gavin.

I pull into my driveway fifteen minutes later and I go inside. I feed Apollo before putting on my pajamas. After I wash my face and brush my teeth, I look at my clock and see it's only 10:00 p.m., so I decide to get into bed and continue reading the current book I'm obsessed with. Apollo joins me and curls into my side. I check to make sure my phone is on full volume and not on vibrate so that I won't miss Gavin's call. With my phone settled next to me on the nightstand, I lie against my pillows and start to read.

Two hours later, the words are starting to blur together and I'm afraid that if I don't go to bed soon, I will be jolted awake by my Kindle smacking me in the face. I put it aside and reach for my phone. Disappointment rears its ugly head as I see how late it is and he hasn't called me back like he said he would.

"Chin up, Aly. Don't waste any pretty breaths on him," I tell myself, repeating the old motto my mother used to say to me when a boy I liked didn't like me back. I turn my light off and settle into the covers, praying that a certain green-eyed devil doesn't occupy my dreams.

Five

GAVIN

I SHOULD'VE NEVER fucking agreed to this.

I didn't have dinner before I got to the Bluebird Cafe, so the idea of grabbing a quick bite to eat with friends when the invitation presented itself sounded like a great idea. I should have known them reassuring me that we'd be quick was a lie, even with most of them having late night studio sessions to get back to. Two hours later, our group of four has turned into a group of ten and we're still sitting at the restaurant. I look around the table at everyone, trying to gauge how much longer they're going to take to finish up so I can pay the bill and get the hell out of here to call Aly back. Everyone is done, but most are still nursing their drinks. I start to feel agitated at the delay, hoping this doesn't diminish what Aly thinks of me. I'm a man of my word, so when I tell someone I'm going to call them back, I do. I look at my watch to see it's midnight.

Screw this. It's time to take matters into my own hands.

"You ready to go, Sos?" I interrupt her conversation with another person and she turns toward me. "If not, no big deal. I can Uber it home."

"We haven't even gotten the check yet," she states while seeing if anyone else got theirs.

I stand up and throw two hundred-dollar bills down to cover me and Sosie, not caring that our bill was nowhere near that amount. "Here's for me and you. I'm gonna head out. Stay and enjoy yourself."

"No, I'll drive you. I'm getting tired anyway." She stands and we say our goodbyes to everyone then walk to the parking lot to Sosie's car.

"Why are you in such a rush to get home?" she asks a couple minutes into our drive, while I'm sending Aly a text, asking if she's still awake.

"Because it's late and I have a long day tomorrow," I reply, and when she glances at me, I can tell she doesn't buy it. "I gotta be in the studio all day tomorrow."

"Yeah, but let me guess the *real* reason you're so anxious to get home."

"Guess away."

"Did you or did you not receive a phone call from one Miss Alyson Dawson?" I look over at her in surprise, since I didn't tell her that she called me. "Oh please, Gavin, don't look so shocked. You've had this goofy, Joker-esque smile on your face ever since she's called. You've also been in your own head the whole night and unusually quiet."

"How do you know her last name?" I ask, suddenly feeling protective of Aly and her privacy.

"It wasn't rocket science. Everyone in that room saw your ogling her all damn night. Plus, I overheard some girls complaining about how unfair it is that all the hot guys in Nashville seem to go for her, yet she's never been seen dating any of them."

"Maybe she's been hurt before and isn't ready to date," I offer, trying to ignore the niggle of irritation in the pit of my stomach at the news that multiple men have gone after her, but then I remind myself that Sos said Aly's never been seen with any of them.

"Or maybe she bats for the other team."

I laugh off Sosie's comment, because there is no fucking way I believe that. "I don't think so," I say confidently. I've never felt such intense sexual tension with another woman, not even my ex.

"Whatever, I just don't get it. She literally called you within ten minutes of you giving her your number. Don't you think that's a little… I don't know, stalkerish? There was zero chase for you."

"Why does there always have to be a chase when you're interested in someone?" I question, not liking where Sosie's line of questioning is headed. "What's the problem? You don't like her? You don't even know her."

"Exactly, Gavin! We don't know her. She could be coo-coo for Cocoa Puffs," she says while glaring at me. "You don't know if she's not completely off her rocker, and yet you're acting like a love-sick puppy!"

"Since when does being interested in someone equal being a love-sick puppy?" I argue, confused by Sosie's obvious anger. "Why are you getting so bent out of shape about me meeting someone?"

"Because last time you met someone, she broke your heart, and I don't ever want to see that pain in your eyes again!" she snaps then presses her lips together. The car goes silent after her confession and I shift in my seat. Shit, she's right. Tori did fuck me up, but she didn't shatter my soul. Looking back, I can now recognize the warning signs for what they were, and I chose to ignore every single one of them.

Then again, Tori's change in personality didn't happen overnight. It was slow at first with her kindness starting to fade. Next, she started going out without me, not wanting to spend time with me, and would only show up when she was wasted and wanted to hook up at the end of the night. When I realized I was only being used for my songwriting skills, it hurt, but it didn't take long for the hurt I was feeling to morph into anger. I don't give a fuck about Tori. I don't even think about her anymore, and that's how I know we weren't truly in love. Because if we were, the end of us would've felt like a thousand little knives stabbing holes into my heart.

Love is magical, torturous, beautiful, and hard. I survived our break-up and actually came out a better man. Being with her taught me exactly what I want for myself and what I expect from any woman I end up with in the future.

"I appreciate you having my back."

She peeks at me out of the corner of her eye, embarrassment coloring her cheeks. I give her shoulder an encouraging squeeze to let her know everything's okay. "But if you don't take risks on people, then you'll end up alone. I've never looked at someone and felt something as strong as I did tonight." I sigh, trying to find the words to describe just how I felt but coming up empty.

Maybe my nervousness tonight was the universe trying to tell me I'm going to meet a girl who's going to turn my world upside down or some cosmic shit like that. Hell, I don't usually believe in that kind of stuff, but I can't help but think that tonight was supposed to happen.

"I love you, Sos, and I honestly don't know what's going to happen, but I do know I'm going to follow my gut and see where it goes."

"I love you too, Gav," she says softly as she wrings her hands on the steering wheel. "And I'm sorry, but I'll always be protective of you. You're like my hero. You really saved my life." My throat gets tight at her words, but I ignore it and smile at her. "And it's because I love you that I'm asking you to go slow with this girl. Maybe just talk to her on the phone for a week, and if that goes good, then plan a date?" She looks at me with worry-filled eyes.

"I can do that." Maybe going slow and talking over the phone first will give me the chance to actually get to know her before we spend any time together.

When we get to the front of my apartment complex, I tell Sosie to take tomorrow off, since my workday will consist of writing songs for other people and hours in the studio. I tell her goodbye then go inside and take the elevator up to the fourteenth floor.

Ten minutes later, I'm pacing the floors of my apartment, questioning whether or not I should call Aly. It's 12:30 in the morning and Aly hasn't replied to my text. On the rest of the car ride home, Sosie filled me in on the information she learned about Aly, which was that she worked for Big Little Music in the A&R department as an assistant. Most people are sleeping at this hour, but when you work in the music business, there are lots of late nights, and oftentimes, that includes partying. If she's a party girl, then whatever I'm feeling will fizzle quickly.

Is that why she hasn't returned my texts? Is she out partying?

Curiosity and jealousy start eating at me as images of her hanging out with other men fill my mind.

"Fuck it, I'm calling her," I say out loud, grabbing my phone from my back pocket and dialing her number. She picks up after the second ring, and I expect to hear loud music and talking, but instead, I'm greeted with complete silence.

"Hello?" I say into the phone, but still no

response. "Aly?"

"Hi," she barely whispers, and guilt floods through me for waking her up.

"Were you sleeping?" *What a fucking stupid question that is, Captain Obvious!* I shake my head at myself, not believing that here I am, an award-winning songwriter, and I can't even think of something normal to say to this girl.

"Uh-huh," she responds back in an almost childlike voice that has me chuckling at how adorable she sounds.

"Darlin', I'm sorry to wake you. I just wanted to keep my promise and call you back. I should've waited until tomorrow. Can I make it up to you by buying you breakfast in the morning?" *Shit*, so much for taking Sosie's advice on taking it slow and talking to her for a week first.

"Mmm-hmm," she mumbles, making me wonder if her short answers might mean she's still asleep.

"Why don't we meet at Star Bagel at eight. Do you know where that is?" I question, thinking that it should be close enough to her job on Music Row that she won't be late for work.

"Uh-huh," she says softly, and I make a mental note to set my alarm thirty minutes early so I can send her a text to remind her about meeting me.

"Sleep tight, darlin', and I'll see you in the morning." With nothing but silence greeting me, I laugh at her lack of response and hang up the phone. I get ready for bed, but the adrenaline coursing through me makes me feel restless. The thought of seeing her again keeps me wide awake and soon, words and sentences start filling my head. With the vision of Aly's gorgeous face on repeat in my brain, I grab my laptop and start putting lyrics together for a new song, one filled with hope and the thought that love might really exist.

Six

ALY

I SMACK THE snooze button on my alarm, groaning at the thought of having to get out of my warm, cozy bed. Today is going to be one of those days I'll be sitting front row on the struggle bus due to lack of sleep. I tossed and turned for most of the night, and for those few hours I did sleep, Gavin occupied my dreams in the most vivid ways.

I shuffle slowly into my kitchen, and I'm barely conscious as I go through my morning routine of starting a pot of coffee and feeding Apollo. Once my fat cat is fed, I get a bowl out of the cupboard for myself and dump way too much cereal in it. I add milk till it hits the brim of the bowl then lean over to sip some off the edge so it doesn't spill when I pick it up. Once the coffee is brewed and poured, I bring my coffee and cereal over to the table, sit down, and start to eat. Just when I'm starting to feel somewhat coherent, my phone dings, alerting me to a text message. I shovel a spoonful of cereal into my mouth before grabbing my phone.

Gavin: Good morning, darlin'! This is your friendly wake-up call to remind you that you agreed to meet me for breakfast at Star Bagel this morning at eight. See you soon!

Cereal and milk starts spewing from my mouth as I choke. *When did I agree to meet him for breakfast?* As soon as I ask myself that I vaguely recall the shrill ringing of my phone in the middle of the night. *That wasn't a dream?*

Shit!

I push back from the table and quickly pour the remainder of my cereal and coffee into the drain of the sink. I shower within five minutes, quickly apply lotion to my body, put on my bra and panties, and then blow dry my hair. I run to my closet to pick an outfit and groan. It figures I have nothing to wear, since I haven't done laundry in over a week. I finally settled on an off-the-shoulder, light-pink mesh sweater with a white tank-top underneath, jeans, and beige-colored peep-toe booties. Once dressed, I apply a little makeup and quickly curl my hair then finalize my look with simple gold jewelry. Knowing it's not going to get any better than this in the time I have, I text Gavin back to tell him I'm on my way then grab my purse and head out the door.

It takes me ten minutes to get to Star Bagel and another five minutes to find parking. Once my tiny car is parked in a spot a couple blocks away, I reapply my lip gloss one more time then take a deep breath to try to calm my shaky nerves. I get out of the car with two minutes to spare and walk down the block to the bagel shop.

I try to think of what kinds of things we can talk about, but all thoughts suddenly vanish from my brain when I spot him waiting outside for me. He's wearing a black shirt that clings like saran wrap to his biceps, gray denim jeans that aren't too tight but fit nicely to his thighs, and stylish black boots. He looks like a professional model leaning against the wall, hands in his pockets, and aviator sunglasses covering his eyes, waiting for his picture to be taken. Nerves start making my belly dance, and I take a couple of deep breaths to calm my racing heart.

Calm down, Aly! He's just a guy you're having breakfast with.

Yeah... a really hot guy you'd like to eat for breakfast.

I watch him take off his sunglasses and push himself off the wall as soon as he sees me coming, his infectious smile brightening my mood. Within seconds, he's standing in front of me, and he startles me when he grabs my hands and pulls me closer. With our bodies only mere inches from touching, I tilt my head back to look up at him. Gah, he's gorgeous, and his green eyes capture my attention. His gaze roams my face, lingering for a moment on my lips before returning to stare into my eyes and what feels like my soul.

"My God, you're stunning."

The first words out of his mouth render me

speechless for a moment and I blush from his compliment.

"Th-thank you and… good morning," I stutter out, not prepared for such an intense greeting. I continue smiling on the outside, but on the inside, I'm cringing at how pathetic I feel and sound.

His mouth curves into a wicked smirk, making me forget my stupidity and my knees almost buckle. "Good morning. You ready to go eat? Because I'm starving," he says while his eyes rake over me, making me question if he's still referring to food when he looks at me that way. I nod and stifle a groan at the loss of his warm hands around mine. Instead, he places one hand on the small of my back to lead me into the restaurant.

Star Bagel is always busy, so we stand in line to place our order. Once that is done, we take our number and look around for a place to sit. As he leads us to the back of the room, I overhear people whispering his name, pointing at him, and taking out their phones to snap pictures. By the time we find an empty table for us to take, I'm nervous for a completely different reason.

"Is it always like this?" I ask, nodding toward two girls standing outside the window, holding their phones to the glass to get a photo of him.

"Not all the time," he replies, and I raise a brow, not believing him. "I try to ignore it or pretend they're admiring some painting on the wall." He looks up, his eyes focusing on whatever is above my left shoulder, and his lips start to twitch. "The masterpiece that is behind you is priceless. I can see why everyone wants to take a photo of it."

I turn around to find a black-and-white portrait of a bulldog with a half-eaten bagel hanging out of his mouth. The photo is so ridiculous we both burst out laughing.

"In fact, I think I need a photo of it." He swiftly takes out his phone, and before I can protest, he's snapping a photo of me with the portrait.

"Beautiful," he says, not even bothering to look down at the picture he just took. I feel my cheeks getting warm again, so I distract myself by taking a sip of water.

"So, tell me all about Aly," he says in a soothing but commanding voice. He sets his forearms on the table and leans forward, his expression attentive as he waits for me to respond.

"What do you want to know?"

"Everything."

"Well," I start, clearing my throat before continuing. "Here's the Cliff's notes, since our time this morning is limited. I was born and raised here in Nashville, graduated from Belmont University, and I currently work at Big Little Music as an A&R assistant."

"That explains why you were at the Bluebird last night," he says with a grin right as the waitress is delivering our food and coffee. "I can't believe you're a native Nashvillian. You guys are becoming like unicorns."

I giggle at his statement, because he's right; this town is booming with transplants and now you can't assume anyone is from here anymore. "Yup, my sister and I are third generation born and raised here. She was the one with me last night."

"The blonde?" he asks with a look of doubt on his face. "You guys don't look anything alike."

"I know," I say with a laugh. "She looks

like our dad and I look like our mom."

"Do you have any other siblings?"

I shake my head before answering. "Just us girls."

"I bet you two have your dad wrapped around your pinky fingers."

My smile falters at his words, because I wish that were the case, but it isn't. No matter how hard I try to hide it, he notices the shift right away. Seeing the concern in his eyes, I decide to give him a small explanation.

"We're closer to our mom than our father. He works a lot and doesn't make himself available to spend time with us." Acknowledging this out loud stings, but I learned a long time ago to not let my father's lack of affection bother me. While I love my father because of who he is, I don't have much respect for how he treats us, especially my sister. I just wish Valerie would go to counseling and learn how to handle it better. She's affected the most by his aloofness toward us.

Understanding replaces his concern and he reaches across the table to grab my hand. "It's his loss, Aly. You understand that, don't you? It's his loss, not yours." He gently squeezes my fingers in encouragement and graces me with a soft smile. The sincerity in his eyes almost has me undone. This man seems to be too good to be true.

Am I still dreaming? I squeeze his hand back to make sure he's not a figment of my imagination and give him an appreciative smile. I loosen my grip as a signal for him to let go of my hand, but instead, he holds onto it.

"Enough about me," I say, wanting to take the attention off me and move it to him. "It's your turn now to tell me everything about you."

"Why don't you tell me what you already know about me and I'll fill in the rest." He raises a mischievous brow before taking a sip of coffee.

"I know you're from Texas and that you're incredibly talented. I know you've made a name for yourself and are now one of the most sought out songwriters in Nashville. So far, you don't seem like you could be a serial killer, but then again, I just met you." I smile, enjoying the sound of his rich, deep laughter. A sound I really hope I get to hear again. "I also know your ex-girlfriend is Tori Langston." I mimic his actions by raising my own brow and lifting my coffee cup to my lips.

His eyes glitter with amusement. "All those things are true. Does it bother you that she's my ex-girlfriend?" He maneuvers our hands so that our fingers are now laced together, his thumb sending shivers down my spine as he caresses the inside of my palm.

I force myself to concentrate and think for a moment on how to answer. "Not at all. She's in your past, right?" For some reason, I need to hear it from him that she's not going to be a threat to whatever this thing is between us.

"She's in my past." He squeezes my fingers once more, and whatever apprehension I felt disappears. He lets my hand go so we can eat but continues speaking. "I grew up in Austin and my mom was the one who introduced me to music, since she got me my first guitar at age eight. Then me and my brother formed our first band two years later," he recalls with a grin. "We called ourselves The Blond Monkeys. Needless to say, we changed the name as we got older and realized how ridiculous that sounded." I smile as he laughs at the memory.

"Does your brother play for your band?" I

ask, because I haven't heard anything about his brother being with him, and last night he was playing solo.

"My brother quit music when his girlfriend unexpectedly got pregnant."

"Oh," I murmur quietly, not knowing what to say. "I'm sorry."

"Don't be. It was for the best; music was never his first love. Baseball was, and then he had his daughter. He currently plays professional ball for the Texas Rangers. He's happy playing ball and being a dad."

"Wow, that's pretty amazing," I say, impressed that his brother is talented with music and baseball. "Did him and his girlfriend get married?"

"No, they didn't. She cheated on him with one of his teammates." His eyes darken in anger, his expression turning cold. "He shares custody of my niece with her."

"I'm really sorry to hear he got hurt by her," I tell him with sincerity. No one deserves to be cheated on. "Do you have any other siblings besides him?"

"No, but Sosie, who you met last night, is more like my sister than my cousin. We grew up together until her parents moved her to California."

I'm about to ask more questions about her, when the alarm from my phone starts to go off and interrupts us.

"Sorry about that," I tell him as I turn it off. "I set an alarm so I wouldn't be late for work. I should get going." I swallow down my disappointment, not wanting our breakfast date to end.

"It was smart of you to set your alarm, 'cause I would stay here all damn day with you if I could." He flashes me a heart-melting smile, and butterflies take flight in my stomach again.

Gah, why couldn't I have won the lottery last week when I played, so I wouldn't have to go to work today?

"I would stay here all day with you too," I admit to him before casting my eyes downward, suddenly feeling shy.

"C'mon, let's get you to work. I'll walk you to your car." He stands and holds out his hand. When he pulls me up, I let him lead me out of the restaurant and take his earlier advice of ignoring the people looking at us. I instead concentrate on his hand holding mine as we casually stroll toward my car, both of us in no rush to part ways.

"This is me," I tell him, nodding at the black Mini Cooper ahead of us. I stop at the trunk and turn around to face him, not wanting to say goodbye.

"Thank you for breakfast," I say, focusing on his shirt before glancing up at him. He doesn't respond with words and instead grabs my arms and pulls me into him, engulfing me in a tight hug. I close my eyes, inhaling his intoxicating scent, hoping it will linger on my clothes long after he's gone.

"You fit perfectly in my arms, like you were made for me." His warm breath tickles my ear, giving me goose bumps.

I open my eyes and lean back to catch his. This man is a master of words, making women swoon with the poetry in his songs. How can I tell if he's being sincere? Talk is cheap, so his actions will determine if he's being real or if he's stringing me along like one of his guitars.

"What are you doing tonight?" His face is so close to mine that the tips of our noses brush. My eyes drop to his lips, and I fight the urge to nip the bottom one.

"I have to work," I murmur, still daydreaming about what those lips might feel like against mine.

"Where?" he softly demands as he tightens his grip.

I look back up into his eyes and notice we are swaying together in a silent dance. Have we been doing this the whole time he's been holding me?

"Exit/In. One of our bands is performing there tonight and I have to be there." I used to think it was cool hanging out with our musicians at every one of their performances, but lately, I'd rather be curled up in bed than having to work another late night. "What are you doing tonight?"

"Looks like I'm going to see a band at the Exit/In."

My eyes widen in surprise that he would want to come see me tonight when he probably has a million other things he could be doing. "Really?"

"Really." He chuckles at my response. "What time should I meet you there?"

"Nine? Do you need me to leave you

passes?" I inquire, but the devilish smirk he rewards me with quickly reminds me of who he is. "Never mind, that was a stupid question, since you can get into anyplace you want to go."

"Not every place. Some places require special permission," he says, his voice making my insides clench. I watch him slowly start to bend his head, and my heart begins pounding in my chest at the realization he's about to kiss me. I close my eyes in anticipation then feel his lips touch the side of my mouth. He loosens his grip around me and slowly lets go of me. I swallow down the disappointment I feel, because dammit, I wanted that kiss!

Good Lord, he's turning me into a hot mess!

"I better let you go before you're late. Text me when you arrive at work so I know you're safe," he demands, and all I can do is nod.

"See you later," I manage to say before walking around to the driver's side and getting in my car. I start the engine, look at the side mirror for oncoming cars, and then ease into traffic. I glance in my rearview mirror and catch him still watching me drive away.

My spine tingles at the thought of seeing

him again. Tonight is going to be a good night; I can feel it. Now, I just have to somehow make it through the day without counting the hours down until I get to see him again.

Seven

GAVIN

AS SOON AS Aly's car disappears from my line of vision, I call Bruce, my recording engineer, to see if he can start working earlier than previously scheduled. In this industry, most of us don't start work until 11:00 a.m. due to the late hours we keep, sometimes not even until after lunch. He doesn't answer, so I leave him a voicemail and send him a text message. Today's session isn't for me but for another artist, so I have to make sure everyone involved can accommodate the schedule change. If not, then I'll just cut the session short if we aren't done by the time I need to leave for the Exit/In. Getting to spend time with Aly tonight is an opportunity I refuse to miss out on, especially with a few out-of-town performances I have coming up.

Breakfast this morning only left me hungry for more time with her. I loved making her laugh, watching the emotions of her facial expressions when talking with her, even when the subject matter turned sad discussing her father and my brother. This morning when I woke up, I thought I imagined those crazy, intense feelings I had last night, but they all came crashing over me the moment I saw her gorgeous smile.

Never once did the conversation feel forced and the only issue was that I struggled to keep my hands to myself. I wanted skin-to-skin contact with her, even if it was just holding her hand. The force of our sexual chemistry almost had me pushing her against her car to devour those lips I so desperately want to taste. Just thinking about all the things I want to do to her makes my cock ache. I'm not alone in my desire; I saw it in her eyes when I was holding her. I know if things continue between us, I won't be able to restrain myself for very long, so hopefully I can prove I'm serious about her.

About us.

I just hope I don't scare her off with my intensity. I don't want to waste time playing games, because first, that's just not how I'm wired. Second, taking things slow means it'll take longer to figure out if she's who I think she is to me. I can tell Aly's guard is up because of my profession, and I get why she'd be more cautious about getting to know me. Then again, if we continue on, we'll both have to prove we're loyal to each other and build the trust that is so necessary to have, especially in this industry.

While walking to my car, I pass a flower shop and go in to send Aly some flowers. Since I don't know what her favorites are, I choose ones that remind me of her: white sunflowers for the happiness she seems to radiate, gardenias for how intoxicating she smells, and calla lilies that represent her beauty. The flowers are perfect for her, and once the florist describes how she'll arrange them, I look up Aly's work address and pay for my purchase, knowing she will love them when they get delivered. I leave the shop and decide I might as well go work out, since I haven't heard back from Bruce. I get into my car and drive to the gym, and as soon as I pull into the parking lot, my cell phone starts ringing with a call from Sosie.

"Are you still at Star Bagel?" she asks before I even get a chance to say hello.

"How did you know I was at Star Bagel?" Dread starts to fill me at the thought of how she found out, since I never told her I was going.

"Pictures of you and Alyson are all over the internet. My phone is ringing off the hook from news stations and reporters asking if I can provide a statement on who the mystery lady you were kissing was."

"*Shit!*" I yell into the phone, angry that I can't even eat a fucking meal out in public anymore. This is the ugly side to fame, where you lose all rights to your privacy. Some people don't care, because they want to be famous, but I'm not that person. It was the main reason why I hesitated releasing "User" on my own, but the idea of someone else singing my story didn't settle well with me. Now, anyone who's with me will pay the price of losing their freedom of anonymity.

Tori loved it when fans and paparazzi took our photo, but Aly seems to be the total opposite with how visibly uncomfortable she was from the attention this morning. I run my hand through my hair in frustration, trying to think of how to respond. "We didn't even kiss on the lips. I kissed her cheek, for fuck's sake."

"Did you get amnesia between last night and this morning? Here's a refresh—you agreed to take things slow by talking to her on the phone first for a week before taking her out on a date. Is this starting to ring a bell at all?" Sosie asks in a chiding, sarcastic tone that starts to grate on my nerves.

"First, watch your tone with me. Second, I know exactly what I said last night—and then I changed my mind, something I have the right to do, because I'm a grown-ass man. I don't need permission to date anyone. So, ask me again if I plan on taking things slow with her," I challenge, because although she can't understand how I feel, she needs to know what my stance on Aly is now that I've seen her again.

"I think I already know what the answer is,

Gavin."

Damn fucking straight. "Be prepared for more phone calls, because I plan to spend more time with her."

She must know by my tone not to argue with me, because the line goes quiet for a moment before she softly replies with a mixture of resignation and worry. "How do you want me to respond to the media?"

"Tell them there's no comment and to respect my damn privacy," I growl, hating we even have to discuss this kind of bullshit. This hasn't been an issue before, but with the popularity of "User" and the hype about my new single fixing to drop, this seems like the new norm of my life.

"Gavin, do you understand that once they find out who she is, they'll probably hound her at work and possibly where she lives?" I nod at the phone, but don't say a word, because she's right; they definitely will. At least with my building, I have the protection of it being locked and a doorman to keep people out. I have no idea if Aly has that same protection.

"Don't get mad at me. I'm only trying to look out for both of you, but maybe you should just cut your ties now before it gets worse. It's not fair to subject her to the kind of scrutiny she's about to endure. Tori was different, since she was already in the limelight, but I don't think Alyson is ready for this."

Her words cause a sharp, sudden pain in my chest, making me refuse to even entertain the idea. "Fuck no, I'm not letting her go unless she tells me she doesn't want to see me," I lie, because even if she did tell me she didn't want to date me, I won't back down. No matter how crazy and insane that thought is, I'm determined to see where this leads.

"Again, you just met this girl. Stop acting like a caveman." Sosie sighs, but I hear a hint of humor in her tone and my lips twitch.

I do feel territorial and possessive of Aly, which is a foreign feeling for me. When Tori would flirt with other men, I would just laugh it off, since she has a flirtatious, narcissistic personality. The thought of Aly flirting with another man makes me feel like I want to punch something.

"I need to go. I know I gave you the day off, but let's meet at my place in two hours to discuss my travel plans before I have to get to the studio."

"Seriously, now I have to meet you on my day off? Some boss you are."

"Go pick up lunch on me from your favorite sushi place and meet at my place," I tell her to soften the blow of having to work on her day off.

"I can do that," she agrees, and I chuckle.

I tell her goodbye and immediately dial Aly to check in with her. Since she's at work, I probably should've just sent her a text, but I want to hear her voice and know she's okay.

"Hey, sorry I didn't call you when I got into the office," she says when she answers. "I was bombarded by my boss as soon as I stepped through the door."

"I just wanted to make sure you got to work okay, baby," I respond, then frown when the phone goes silent. "You still there?"

"Yeah," she responds quietly.

"What was that about?"

"You."

"Me?" Worry fills the pit of my stomach.

"I'm just not used to being called 'baby' and 'darlin'.'"

I smile. "Start getting used to it. I have

more good ol' Texas terms of endearments up my sleeve, sweet cheeks." My smile broadens as her whimsical laughter fills my ears.

"We'll see," she says, sounding serious after her laughter dies down and she clears her throat. "My boss told me there are photos of us from breakfast all over the Internet already. Did you know about that?"

"Sosie just called to tell me. I'm really sorry about that. I wish we could've eaten in peace. Is that what your boss bombarded you with?"

"Yes, the photos were sent to him by one of our marketing assistants, who follows country music gossip. They didn't mention my name, but she recognized me and emailed the link to him."

"You're not in trouble, are you?" The last thing I would want is for her job to be in jeopardy because of her association with me.

"No, I didn't get in trouble, but do I need to be concerned that this is going to happen every time I'm out with you?"

My intuition on her not liking the attention was obviously spot on. *Fuck.* I grip my steering wheel harder, hating the worry in her voice.

"I'd like to tell you this won't happen every time we're together, but I can't control when people take our photo and post it to social media," I tell her, wishing we weren't having this conversation less than twenty-four hours after we just met. "Listen, I'm asking that you take a chance on me. I want to get to know you and spend more time with you. I know you're hesitant about me, but I also know you're feeling this insane chemistry we have." Hearing her little sigh, I continue my argument. "I want to properly date you, and we can go at whatever speed you're comfortable with. Just know that whenever you're with me, I promise I'll keep you safe," I vow, hoping she believes me. I understand the consequences of dating someone in the spotlight. I just hope she thinks I'm worth the risk.

Silence fills the line for a brief moment before I hear her whisper, "Okay."

"Okay," I say, smiling like a fool. "I'll see you tonight, darlin'. Call me if you need anything."

"I will. Later, Gavin." Her tone is breathy and seductive, and I hope I get to hear that again when I'm close enough to kiss her.

I reluctantly hang up and shake off the images filling my mind. I grab my workout bag, exit my car and head into the gym, needing to exert the adrenaline that thoughts of Aly provoke.

I DRIVE ACROSS town agitated, because I'm late and pissed that my time with Aly will now be limited due to work. My session with Bruce was productive, but we still need a couple more hours to finalize the song we're working on. Knowing I had to be somewhere, everyone agreed to take a two-hour dinner break and come back to finish up. It sucks that it's going to be another late night, but seeing Aly will make it worth it.

I pull into the parking lot behind the building and walk up to the bouncer sitting at the back entrance. Aly texted earlier to thank me for the flowers and to tell me she went ahead and put me on the VIP list, just in case I had trouble getting in. I've been to the Exit/In numerous times and know the manager, so I could probably get in on my own. But this is Aly's gig, so I decide to follow protocol. I show the bouncer my ID, and he places a band around my wrist then opens the door to let me in.

Like the Bluebird Cafe, the Exit/In is a small, intimate venue rich with history. Famous musicians from all types of genres have performed here, and it's another Nashville musical institution. Unlike the Bluebird Cafe, being loud is encouraged here, as it's a true rock n' roll concert venue with zero seating. The stage is elevated high, so there isn't a bad view no matter where you stand.

I walk through the small hallway and arrive at the back of the stage. The place is completely packed, and the crowd is dancing along with the music. I look around and spot Aly leaning against the wall on the side of the stage, watching who I'm assuming are her clients. My heart pounds as I walk toward her, and when she spots me, she smiles, stealing my breath away. It takes every ounce of willpower not to grab her hand and find the nearest closet to devour her in. Instead, I engulf her in a tight embrace and nuzzle my nose into the crook of her neck.

The smell of her floral perfume sends

my senses into overdrive, making my jeans uncomfortably tight. I pull back to look at her and am rewarded with a sheepish grin that showcases a small dimple I want to kiss. I reluctantly let go of her when she turns in my arms to introduce me to one of her co-workers. The band is so loud, I can barely hear what the girl's name is. Aly holds up her cell phone and motions for me to grab mine so she can send me a text message.

Aly: It's so loud in here. Let's go next door and grab a bite to eat.

Me: Great idea, I'm starving!

She smiles as she reads my text then waves at her co-worker and mouths, *I'll be back in an hour*, before grabbing my hand and pulling me back out the door I just walked through.

"Is next door okay for you?" she asks, looking up at me once we can finally hear each other talk. "I can't be too far away, since I need to be back for their finale."

"I don't care where we go, as long as I'm with you," I answer, watching her cheeks turn an adorable shade of pink.

"Okay." She ducks her head in shyness, making me smile.

I give her hand a squeeze then lead her to the restaurant next door that is owned by the same owners of the Exit/In. We're seated immediately despite the crowd of college students mixed with young professionals who occupy the bar. The waitress comes by with waters and we both order a beer while looking over the menu that consists of mostly burgers and Americanized Mexican food.

"Have you eaten here before?" I ask, wondering what her favorite food is. I'm hoping I can get a clue of where I should take her for our first official date.

"Anytime we have a show here, I stop in and get the nachos. They're delicious." She closes her menu and smiles at me.

"I'm assuming by your gorgeous smile that you're getting that again?" I grin as she nods like an excited child waiting for her favorite ice cream. "Is Mexican your favorite kind of food?"

"Yes, but I just love food in general." She shrugs, causing the wide neck of her sweater to droop down the side of her shoulder.

My eyes lock on the small glimpse of her smooth, beautiful flesh and I suddenly wonder how her skin would taste and what her reaction would be if I ran my tongue up her shoulder to her neck. I silently groan and adjust myself underneath the table. *Focus,* I tell myself and force my eyes back to hers.

"Have you been to Texas? Tex-Mex is the best outside of having food in Mexico."

"I haven't been to Texas... or out of the country yet." She laughs at the surprised look on my face. "The only place our parents ever took us to was Disney World, and I don't even remember that. My sister and I always talk about taking off work and backpacking Europe together, but we haven't had the chance yet."

"We're definitely going to rectify that. You tell me when you can get off and we'll go to Texas. I am due for a trip home soon. Maybe we can go somewhere out of the country before my tour starts." My mind starts racing at possible dates when I notice her looking at me funny.

"Do you always bring strange women that you just met home?" she teases, but I don't miss that flash of concern in her eyes.

"I'm hoping you won't be a strange woman by the time you meet my family," I tell her, watching intently to see how she reacts to my words. *If things progress with us, would she even want to meet my family?* Tori was never interested in going to Texas with me. She always had an excuse anytime I brought it up, so eventually, I stopped asking.

"You're kind of intense," she says quietly after a long moment, not giving anything away with her expression or tone.

"Does that scare you?" I question with a raised brow. Obviously, I don't want her scared, but I want her to know how serious I am.

"No." The word is soft before she starts biting her bottom lip. "I actually kind of like it."

Fuck, this woman is going to make me take her to my car and see how far I can get with her in the backseat if she keeps staring at me like this. Thankfully, the waitress shows up with our drinks and breaks our trance. We place our food order and once she leaves, I decide to change the subject so I don't look like a madman carrying her out of here.

"What else do you have to do tonight for work?"

"Besides making sure the band doesn't trash the dressing room, nothing much," she jokes with a smile. "I just need to check in with the band to see how they felt tonight went, talk with the manager about final ticket sales, and then report in with my boss tomorrow. Normally, I wouldn't need to stick around, but one of our newer employees is with me tonight, so that's why I need to get back before the band ends. I'm sorry you have to hang with me while I work."

"I'm not sorry." I give her a reassuring smile. "Did you always want to work in the music industry?" I'm always curious why people choose this business. Sure, it can be made to appear glamorous on TV or in magazines, but most people who work on stage or behind the scenes know you work like a dog in an attempt to make a name for yourself.

"I've loved music since I was a child, but I can't play an instrument or sing for the life of me." She laughs, captivating me with the sparkle in her eye. "When I had to decide what I wanted to do when I grew up, I thought combining music and taking care of people would be the perfect job, but I don't think being an A&R assistant fits that description."

"It's not easy getting into this business, so obviously, you impressed your bosses. Don't sell yourself short. You're in the perfect job, because you do help artists with their career."

"Thanks, but lately it just hasn't felt very satisfying. I don't know…" She looks away. "I've just been questioning if I made the right career choice." Understanding the lost look in her expression, I wish we were sitting next to each other so I could hold her, but instead, I do the next best thing and reach for her hand to squeeze it.

"One hundred percent, you made the right career choice. I mean, are you or are you not sitting here with me now?" I joke, hoping to see that sparkle back in her eyes.

She smiles then rolls her eyes. "I guess you're right."

"I know I am." I lift her hand and kiss her fingers then ask, "Are most of your clients in the rock genre?"

She casts her eyes down and gives me a shy smile while peeking at me through her lashes. "Even though I listen to all types of music, classic and indie rock are my favorites. My boss likes to keep me happy, so he lets me take care of our clients in those genres."

"Do you like anyone in country music?" I release her hand and sit back to cross my arms over my chest, narrowing my eyes at her in a teasing manner. Her eyes follow my movements and linger a little bit on my biceps before moving up to my face.

"Some," she says hesitantly, making me question if she really does or if she's just saying that to amuse me.

"Name them," I challenge and bite the inside of my cheek to keep from laughing out loud at her exasperated look. I can see the wheels in her head start to turn as she attempts to name someone, and I know in that instant country music is probably her least favorite genre.

"Keith Urban!" she says loudly in excitement, pride shining in her eyes for remembering his name.

"Do you only know of him because he's married to a famous actress you like?" I question, trying not to laugh.

"No, I actually like him. One of my favorite songs by him is 'Somebody Like You.' It also helps that he's cute and Australian. Accents are kinda my thing." She winks, causing me to swallow down the uncomfortable pain I'm in from how hard she's got me. Thank God the waitress arrives at that moment. We both eye each other's order then dig in, picking off one another's plate while we continue talking. Before we know it, the hour is up and it's time for us to leave, so I pay the bill, grab Aly's hand, and escort her out of the restaurant.

"I had a really great time tonight," I tell her, bringing her small hand up to my mouth to kiss her knuckles as we stroll back toward the Exit/In.

"Me too." Her smile is small and shy as we walk in silence. I glance down at her, noticing that pink has spread up her cheeks as the sexual tension radiates between us.

"Are you leaving?" she questions when I stop next to my truck. I nod, and disappointment screams from her eyes, making me feel like a fucking asshole for having to leave her.

"I have to go back to the studio tonight. We didn't get to finish the song we were working on. We're close, so it should only be a couple more hours."

"You weren't done working?" Her gaze fills with surprise. "Gavin, you didn't have to meet me tonight. We could have met up tomorrow." She attempts to let go of my hand and tries to take a step back, but I refuse to let go of her. I grab her wrist and haul her up against me, wrapping my arms around her so she can't escape.

"I didn't want to wait until tomorrow to see you again." I feel her arms close around my waist, her touch sending warm sensations up my spine. I can't help the low groan that escapes when I watch her gently bite her bottom lip again.

"You're so beautiful," I murmur while memorizing the shape of her face and those warm eyes of hers that I know will haunt my dreams. I push a piece of her hair behind her ear and lightly caress her cheek. Her eyes lock on mine, and I can tell she's searching for something—for what, I don't know, but whatever it is, I want her to find it within me. I feel her squeeze me tighter, and listen to her breath coming out faster as her gaze travels down to my lips.

"Kiss me, Gavin," she demands in a

whisper, her pupils dilated and filled with desire.

I growl my approval and don't hesitate, snaking one of my hands up her spine, grabbing her by the back of her neck, and crashing my mouth onto hers. This kiss is the opposite of soft and slow; it's rough and hungry, our passion for each other undeniable in this moment. Hot waves of desire roll through me every time her tongue touches mine, making me crave more. She's my new drug of choice and her high is one I never want to come down from. Her hands move up my chest to my hair, tugging and pulling as we try to get as close to each other as possible. When she moans, I groan in response, the sound of us devouring each other filling the air around us, drowning out the music coming from inside the building.

A very small part of me is screaming to stop, reminding me that we're at one of her events and anyone can find us out here behind my truck. I start to slow our kiss down, and eventually, I find the strength to break away. But I can't resist trailing kisses down her jaw to her neck, nipping and licking every inch until I reach that patch of deliciously exposed skin at her shoulder I'd been eyeing at dinner.

"I knew you were going to taste this amazing, baby. I can't wait to explore and try the rest of you," I whisper against her ear before nibbling on her lobe. I feel her shiver as she moves her head back, urging me to reclaim her mouth. As soon as my mouth touches hers, her lips part and our tongues dance together in what feels like pure ecstasy. Her little moans only stoke the fire still burning, and I'm once again lost in the abyss that is Alyson Dawson.

I force her to walk backward until her back hits a car that's not mine. She opens her legs and wraps her arms around me, like she's trying to mold her body to mine. My hands start roaming down those dangerous curves of hers, stopping over her delicious ass. Before I can stop myself, I hoist her up and she automatically wraps her legs around my waist. The heat of her rubs against my cock through our clothes, and the car I have her against begins to move.

Fuck, I can't get enough of her.

I can't stop kissing, tasting her, touching her.

Her moaning gets louder, her breath coming

out in little pants. I know if we keep this up, she's going to come from the friction against her clit. The selfish bastard in me wants to put my hand down the front of her pants and rub her until she screams out my name. I'm about to listen to my wicked inner voice when someone else makes the decision for me.

"What the hell? Get off of my car!" a man shouts, breaking our spell. I put her down and she immediately buries her face against my chest.

"Sorry about that, sir," I say as I grab her hand and walk to the back entrance of the building.

"Crap, I gotta go. I think the show's over."

She's probably right, since I can't hear the band any longer and more people are now exiting the building. I pull her in for a hug and swiftly kiss her lips.

"Call me when you get home tonight," I demand, and she nods slowly, still in a daze. I smile at her smugly, enjoying seeing those swollen lips and heated cheeks, knowing that came from me. "You better get going before I continue what we started in front of all these people."

"You better continue what you started," she says with a wicked smile that makes me laugh. "Text me when you get to the studio, so I know you got there okay."

"Will do, baby," I agree as she backs up a step.

"See you soon."

"You bet you will," I reply before she blows me a kiss and turns on her heel, disappearing into the crowd.

Once I can't see her anymore, I take a shaky breath and go to my car. I sit in the parking lot of the Exit/In and reflect on what just happened between us and can only hope she's not too good to be true.

Eight

ALY

I SPEED LIKE a maniac into the parking lot of my office, my tires squealing as I hastily pull into the first open spot I find. I put the car into park and pull down my visor to check my appearance in the mirror.

"Shit," I groan out loud as I take in the disheveled hair, swollen lips, and dilated eyes. Not to mention the purple bags that no foundation can cover up. I look and feel like a hot mess, and it's all because of a certain green-eyed devil I've become hypnotized by.

Gavin was still at the studio last night when I got home, so it wasn't until midnight when he called to say goodnight and we stayed up for another hour talking. Before hanging up, I agreed to meet him for breakfast this morning, since Shane usually lets his employees come into work late when we have work events the night before. We met at a tiny, hole-in-the-wall restaurant he knew about on the east side of downtown Nashville. The place wasn't very crowded, and it was nice not having our photo taken by strangers. We had the chance to get to know a little more about each other, and during our conversation, Gavin told me all about his upcoming trip to Los Angeles, where he's scheduled to perform on a couple of late-night talk shows.

Once we were done eating, he paid for our bill and walked me to my car. What was supposed to just be a quick kiss on the lips turned into a full-blown make-out session in his truck, which was conveniently parked right next to my car. I start to get heated all over again just thinking about where I let his lips and hands roam. If it wasn't for the incoming call from Willow, I probably would have had an orgasm in his truck from the deliciously naughty things he was doing to my body.

I don't even remember how his hands got underneath my dress—then again, one small touch of his lips and I'm a goner. I fall a little further down the rabbit hole for Gavin McNeer each time we're together, and I know there's going to come a point when I won't be able to get back out of it. We were being reckless, as anyone could've seen us despite his windows being heavily tinted. But worrying about what we were doing was the last thing on either of our minds.

Good Lord, that man has cast a spell over me! I shake my head at myself and the wanton behavior that comes out every time he touches me. I grab my makeup bag out of my purse and add some powder and blush then apply some lipstick and try to run a brush through the tangles his hands created in my hair. I take a deep breath, satisfied with my handiwork, and exit the car. My phone starts ringing while walking toward the building, and I pull it out of my purse to see Willow is calling me again. She's relentless when she doesn't hear from me, and if I ignore her call one more time, she'll show up at my office unannounced.

"Hey pretty lady, what's up?" I chirp in an

overly bright tone as I pull open the front door to my office building and head in.

"What's up? Seriously? My so-called best friend has been sucking face with the hottest country singer in town and doesn't even tell me! I have to read it on the Internet." Guilt washes over me as I hear the anger in her voice. "You have a lot of explaining to do, Dawson, and I don't care that you're at work right now. Wait, are you even at work right now?"

"Yes, I'm at work," I confirm, but purposely leave out that I just walked through the doors.

"Great! Start talking."

"Willow, I'm sorry, but you know my office is a cubicle and anyone can hear me." I lower my voice as I pass by my co-workers, not wanting them to hear my conversation. "I promise I'll call you back later."

"Nope, not happening. I'll see you on your lunch break and you can tell me then."

I reach my desk and plop myself down in my chair. "I have a lot of work to do today and am not sure I can leave. I promise I'll call you when I get out of here this evening."

"I'll bring food and we can eat there. Text me where you want me to pick up food from."

I roll my eyes at her persistence and wish she would just trust me to call her later. It's not like I have a track record for not calling her back. She's usually the one who doesn't call me back right away. "You're being ridiculous."

"But am I though?"

"Yes, you are."

"Who ya talking to?" a voice behind me asks, startling me to the point that my phone goes crashing to the floor. I turn around to see Shane perched at the edge of my desk, arms crossed over his chest with an evil smile on his face.

"I was talking to Willow, Shane. Jesus, you scared me!"

"Hello? Aly? You better not have hung up on me!" we hear Willow threaten through the phone as I pick it up off the ground.

"Hi, Willow!" Shane says loud enough for her to hear. "Aly, bring the phone conversation into my office so we can all talk on speaker."

"But this isn't a work-related phone call," I reply, not liking the sparkle of mischief I see in his eyes. There's no way I want to give both of them the opportunity to hound me about Gavin at the same time.

"Was your phone conversation going to be about Gavin?" Before I can tell him no, Willow screams yes so loudly into the phone that I have to hold it away from my ear. Shane hears her response and smiles. "Gavin's a musician and we're in the music business, so —" Shane winks. "—it's a work-related call."

"That's complete garbage and you know it! He's not even signed to our label," I argue against his ridiculous logic. All Shane wants to do is find out how far I've gone with Gavin, and I prefer not to talk about that with my boss, no matter how close we are.

"In my office now, Alyson!" he commands with a serious look on his face before turning on his heel and marching inside his office. I wish he could feel the daggers I'm shooting at his back with my eyes.

"I love that man," Willow says, and I can't help but snort at her comment. Willow says she loves anyone who's willing to be her partner in crime when it pertains to ganging up on me.

"Hold on," I grumble out to her while I reluctantly walk to his office and shut the door. I take a seat in front of his desk, place my phone down in between us, and turn the speakerphone on.

"There, now you two can gossip with each other in front of me," I say sarcastically and lean back into the chair, silently praying for some patience in dealing with these two today.

"Okay, Willow, what was she updating you on with Gavin? Because I haven't gotten an update on the situation since yesterday morning."

I groan and Shane sticks out his tongue at me while he waits for Willow to respond. I love how my dating life is now called "the situation."

"I haven't gotten any updates at all! She never even told me about meeting him." Shane looks at me in surprise, his mouth open so wide that wasps could use that big hole to make a nest.

"Sounds to me like someone is being a horrible best friend," Shane tells her while eyeing me in mock disgust. "I'll fill you in on how they met, since I happened to be there." He clears his throat and moves closer to the phone in order for her to hear him better.

I lean forward to chime in, so she doesn't believe all the nonsense I know he's going to spew. "Let me just warn you, Willow, that this will be a full-blown exaggeration and nothing like the reality of what happened."

"You hush. I'm telling the story!" Shane waves me off as if I'm some little gnat annoying him. "Now, where do I begin?" He rubs his hands together. "It was industry night at The Bluebird Cafe and Gavin was there performing on behalf of his record label. As soon as he sat down and took one look at our beautiful Miss Aly, he was smitten." He bats his eyelashes at me.

"Here we go." I sigh. I seriously think he gets high off of meddling in other people's lives.

"It's my story to tell," he says, and Willow laughs, making him smile even broader. "So as soon as he saw our girl, the air in the room got heated under the intensity of his gaze while he stared at her. Our little Aly apparently felt the same way about him, because for the next ten minutes, they just stared at each other as if they were telepathically having sex."

I shake my head at him, my lips twitching at hearing Willow's laughter again. "This is so ridiculous," I say to myself, since I know neither of them are listening to me.

"When Gavin's set ends, he hands Aly his card and tells her to call him—in front of everyone! Valerie was with us too, and being the boring, older sister she is, she naturally told Aly not to call him."

"Hey, that's not nice. My sister's not boring!" I cut in, not letting even my boss talk badly about my sister.

"Oh c'mon now, you know I love Valerie, but she's a CPA for Pete's sake. They're boring!" I wouldn't call Valerie boring, but because she rarely ever comes out with us, Shane considers her an old fuddy-duddy. "Anyway, Aly listened to her intuition and called him that night. It has been thirty-six hours since then, and they've seen each other for breakfast and dinner." Shane pauses and studies me intently, his eyes starting at the top of my head and going all the way down to my feet. "And judging with how she looks right now, he might have eaten her for breakfast this morning."

My mouth drops open in shock, my cheeks reddening at the fact that Shane was able to tell I messed around with Gavin.

He throws back his head and laughs at my expression. "Oo-wee, Willow, you should see the permanent blush staining Aly's cheeks right about now."

I groan and throw my face into my hands, wanting to hide from the insanity that has suddenly become my life.

"Please tell me you haven't had sex with him already?" Willow questions in concern.

"No, of course not!" I say then see Shane raise a brow, and I start to get annoyed and angry with the double standard the world has created with men being able to have sex on the first date, but it's unacceptable for women to do the same. "And by the way, even if I had already slept with him, that would be no one's business but my own."

"Aly, you know I would never judge you even if you did sleep with him already, but this is no ordinary guy you're dating. You're dating someone who's famous, a guy who just wrote a hit song about being used by his ex-girlfriend."

"Not to mention, he's scrumdiddlyumptious hot and has women throwing themselves at him all the time," Shane chimes in, and I give him the death glare for having to remind me about Gavin's popularity with the female population.

"Nice, Shane, real nice," Willow says sarcastically before continuing on. "All I'm saying is to please be careful with this guy. What exactly are you looking for with him?"

"I don't know. You know I wasn't really looking to get into a relationship with anyone," I reply, speaking to Willow like Shane isn't even in the room. "Not that I was being closed-minded to dating, but I can't do casual and I have no interest in spending time with people I don't feel a connection with. Honestly, he's the first guy I actually want to spend time with." Talking about him gets my heart racing, and I imagine his handsome face. "He's super intense and completely overwhelms me in a good way. He makes me feel wanted, and when he tells me how beautiful he thinks I am, I actually believe it." I bring my gaze back to Shane, who sighs loudly with a dreamy look on his face while cupping his chin in his hands. "I don't know; there's something about him, and my heart is telling me to give him a chance."

"Wow," Willow says after a couple moments of silence. "Well, I think you need to listen to your intuition if you're feeling that strongly about him. I'm happy that you've found someone you think might be worthy of you, because you're pretty damn special, Alyson Dawson."

"Amen, sister!" Shane yells with excitement and winks at me. "So far, Gavin's reputation has been squeaky clean, and you know I'll be keeping my ears open if I hear of anything otherwise."

"I love you guys. Despite my annoyance with you both, I'm pretty damn lucky to call you my squad," I say with a laugh.

"So… when do I get to meet him?" Willow asks, and I wonder the same thing, since Gavin's schedule for the next week is pretty busy.

"He leaves for Los Angeles tomorrow and won't be back for a couple days, which puts us into next week." Even though I know this tiny break will be a good test for us, the thought of not seeing him makes me sad.

"You're meeting him next Thursday, Willow," Shane informs us, and I look at him in confusion, wondering if he knows something I don't. "We have the suite for the Predators game next week. I'll give you four tickets. Take Gavin and Willow and use the last one for whomever else you want to invite."

"That's really generous of you, Shane, but I don't know his schedule for next week." I know he will be back on Monday, but we haven't discussed what the rest of his week looks like.

"Text him and ask," Shane counters, nodding at the phone.

"I'll text him about it later."

"Do it now, Aly!" he demands.

"God, you're bossy today! Willow, hold on a second please," I say in exasperation as I pick up my phone and proceed to text Gavin.

Me: Are you free next Thursday to go to the Predators game with me and my best friend, Willow? You can bring along Sosie or whomever you want. I have one extra ticket for the suite we'll be in. I completely understand if you can't.

I hit Send and stick my tongue out at Shane. "There, you happy now?"

"No, let me see the proof that you actually

asked him." Before I can react, Shane grabs the phone out of my hands and looks at my text messages.

"Hey! That's rude!" I stand up and try to grab it back from him, but Shane just moves to hold it above his head. With him being taller than me and his desk between us, I don't stand a chance of retrieving it from him. I angrily stomp my foot and glare at him as I sit back down. "I'm over you, Adams!"

"Please don't kill him yet, because I actually would like to go to a Predators game for free." Willow laughs.

The wheels in my head start to turn, as next week will be the perfect time to introduce her to Brodie. "Even if Gavin can't make it, we'll still go," I reassure her, silently plotting how to introduce those two that night. I'll have to let Brodie know I'll be there, and hopefully, he'll be able to meet us after the game.

My scheming is interrupted when my phone buzzes with a text message notification. Shane doesn't even bother handing my phone back to me and instead takes it upon himself to read the message first. His lips form a sly smile, and that I'm-up-to-no-good sparkle in his eye returns.

"According to Gavin's text message, and I quote, 'I'll rearrange my schedule to be with you. Count me in,' end quote." Shane hands back my phone with a sigh and a satisfied grin on his face.

"Damn, that's hot," Willow remarks, and I nod in complete agreement.

I've been very impressed with Gavin and his efforts to make sure we see each other at least once a day since meeting. And even then, he's constantly texting and calling me throughout the day.

"Great, it's a date then! I look forward to meeting Mr. Sexy-as-Sin McNeer next week," Willow says, and I know she's smiling. I can't help but smirk, knowing Gavin's not the only good-looking guy she's going to meet that night. I know Brodie will definitely like what he sees when he meets Willow, because she's gorgeous. But will the feeling be mutual? I don't have a very good track record with setting Willow up, since she has such high standards when it comes to men. I just have a feeling that if she gives Brodie a chance, my matchmaking skills will finally pay off.

Nine

GAVIN

I RUB MY eyes with the heels of my hands, tiredness seeping through my body as I leave the studio for the night. Today turned out to be longer than I expected, with getting ready for our television appearances in LA and coming back to the studio to write with seasoned country music star Patty Douglas. I probably should've declined her last-minute invite to join her and gone home to pack, but something told me to go and I'm glad I did.

We got the first draft of a song done within two hours, which is pretty damn impressive. I have a feeling the final production of this song is going to smoke the country music charts and possibly the Billboard charts as well. I believe in this song so much that I even promised her I would continue working on it while in LA. Some songs you know right away are going to be a hit and this is one of them.

When I get in my car and close the door, I smell that sweet scent that's been plaguing me all day long. I inhale deeply, moaning out loud as remnants of Aly's perfume tickle my senses. My fingers start twitching at the memory of being inside her warm, slick pussy. I had no intention of going as far as I did inside my truck in broad daylight this morning, but things escalated quickly when her soft, plump lips touched mine. Her kisses send me spiraling out of control, and I completely lose myself when I'm with her.

Do these intense feelings scare the crap out of me? Hell yeah, they do, but despite the craziness of feeling this way over someone I just met, it also has never felt more right. I start my engine and look at the clock on my dashboard to see it's past eleven and she might be sleeping. An overwhelming need to see her one more time before my flight in the morning rocks me. I can't stand the idea of not seeing her for three days. I grab my cell phone and call her.

"Hey," she answers softly, and I immediately smile at hearing her voice.

"Hey, darlin', did I wake you?"

"No, I was just reading... and maybe waiting up for just a little bit longer in hopes to hear from you," she admits with a nervous giggle, and my heart hammers in my chest at how fucking sweet she is.

"I'm sorry it took so long, baby. I've been thinking of you all damn day though. How about something even better than a phone call? Are you up for a late-night visitor?" I ask, hoping she wants to see me as badly as I want to see her. Seconds tick by without her response, and my hope starts to fade.

"Sure," she finally says. "But if your plan is to get laid tonight, then maybe you shouldn't come over," she states coldly, her voice lacking its usual warm tone.

I draw my eyebrows together in concern at her sudden change in demeanor. *Where the hell is this coming from?*

"Do you think the only reason I want to see

you tonight is to have sex?" I question, my own voice sounding cold.

"No," she replies hesitantly. "Maybe... I don't know." She sighs and I let out the breath I didn't realize I was holding. I'm glad she was honest, because if we're going to build trust in this relationship, then she needs to always tell me any doubts she's feeling.

"First off, thank you for sharing your doubts with me. Please don't ever hesitate to express them. Secondly, of course I want to fuck you, Aly, but that's not my first priority," I tell her in a firm voice, needing to erase any thoughts of me just wanting her for sex out of her head. "I want to get to know you, and the rest will come when you're ready. Doesn't matter how long that takes."

"Are you really this perfect?" she asks, her question making me chuckle.

"I'm far from perfect. No one's perfect, and I'm sure I'll do something in the future to piss you off. I'm just going to apologize right now for that. Hope you'll remember this conversation when it eventually does happen." She laughs and I take that as an indication she's feeling better. "Honestly, I just wanted to see you one more time before I leave tomorrow. Cuddling and sleeping was all I was thinking about, and it's perfectly okay if you tell me that I shouldn't come over tonight."

"Cuddling and sleeping sound good to me," she says in her soft, sweet voice that makes my chest tighten with want.

"Are you sure about this?" I question, not wanting her to invite me over out of obligation.

"Positive."

"All right, then. Text me your address and I'll see you in a few." We say goodbye and within seconds, she sends me her address. I put it into my navigation and am pleasantly surprised to see she's less than five miles away from me. I put the car into reverse, back out of my parking space, and start driving to her house.

Ten minutes later, I'm pulling into the driveaway of a cute, cottage-style house. The house is located in an older, trendy neighborhood that is close to Belmont University and near Music Row. Even though this house is small and close to thirty years old, because of the area it's in, it's worth a lot of money. Questions of how she can afford to live here bubble up into my mind while I walk to the front door.

The landscaping is well kept with trimmed bushes and beautiful flower beds. The front porch looks inviting with potted plants and a swing located to the right of the front door. Before I can get to the first step of the porch, the outside light turns on and the door swings open. Aly stands in the doorway, wearing a long-sleeved, pink V-neck shirt and pajama pants with hearts all over them. Her long hair is down, falling over her shoulders and framing her beautiful, makeup-free face.

"How did you know it was me?" I ask as she moves aside and lets me in. I turn around to face her while she closes the door and locks it.

"I heard your car door shut." She walks up to me, and I embrace her in a tight hug. We stand like this for a moment, her head resting against my chest, and I have no doubt she can hear the pounding of my heart.

"This place is nice," I whisper as I take in the Bohemian-styled living room that fits Aly's personality. Her cream-colored walls have colorful artwork hanging on them, with a large, round gold-rimmed mirror above her fireplace mantle. A navy-blue sectional couch is against the main wall with gold-and-white accent pillows on it. Her hardwood floors are covered in Turkish-style accent rugs that are strategically placed around the house. She has an open floor plan, so my eyes wander over to the updated white-and gray-kitchen with a small breakfast nook perfect for four people. Despite the older look of the exterior of the house, the inside has been completely remodeled and updated.

"Thanks, but why are you whispering?" She leans back in my arms and gives me a funny look.

"I don't want to be disrespectful and wake up your roommate."

"Roommate? I don't have a roommate." My arms drop to their sides in shock, giving her the perfect opportunity to step back and walk around me to the kitchen. "Do you want something to drink?"

"Hold up, did you just say you don't have a roommate?" My voice must have come across as angry, because her eyes widen in surprise.

"That's right," she says slowly, confusion

written all over her face. "I don't have a roommate. Is there a problem with that?"

"You're telling me you live in this house all by yourself? Alone?" The idea of Aly being here all by herself every night with no one to protect her in case of a burglary makes my blood start to boil.

"Technically, I'm not alone. I have Apollo." She bends down and picks up her huge white furball of a cat and scratches behind his ear. The cat starts to purr but continues to size me up with his eyes.

"Cute, but you need real protection." I walk over to the living room windows and am appalled to see that anyone can see in when she has her curtains drawn open. "How do you feel about a dog?" If she says she loves them, I'm buying her a German Shepherd tomorrow.

"You're not getting me a dog, Gavin. I have an alarm system and cameras all around the house. I live in a good neighborhood and know all my neighbors. We all look out for each other."

"I don't like the idea of you by yourself here. Anyone can walk in from the street, throw a brick through these windows and they're in."

I wave my arm around the living room, hoping she can see my point of view on this. "I think you need to consider leaving this place." Aly's already told me she thinks I'm intense. If she knew I was entertaining the idea of moving her into my apartment with me, she would tell me I need to be institutionalized.

"I've lived here for over four years now. If anyone is leaving, it's going to be you if you don't drop this bullshit." She puts the cat down, crosses her arms over her chest, and glares at me with that I'm-done-talking-about-this-and-so-are-you stare. I clench my jaw in aggravation at her stubbornness, but I'm also completely turned on by how hot she looks when she's angry. Not to mention her cursing sounds so naughty coming from that sweet little mouth of hers. I mentally count to ten before approaching her. I place my hands gently on her shoulders and squeeze.

"Do you at least have a gun hidden somewhere for protection?" She rolls her eyes and shoves my hands off of her, turns on her heel, and walks to the kitchen. "Answer me, Aly," I demand when she continues to ignore me.

"You're really annoying me right now with this," she tells me with a scowl on her face. "Yes, Gavin, I have a gun, but I hate it and don't ever want to use it."

Thank fuck for that. I let out a sigh of relief, which just seems to annoy her even more. She turns her back toward me, grabs a glass from her cupboard, and gets herself some water.

I cautiously approach the kitchen, knowing that I'm now skating on thin ice and need to drop the subject. I'll figure out how to handle this on my own while I'm out in Los Angeles. "Darlin', I'm just concerned for your safety." I walk to her and place my hands on her waist, turning her so she faces me. She doesn't hug me back and looks down into her water. I grab her chin and tip it up, forcing her to meet my eyes. "The thought of anything happening to you drives me insane with fear. Are you going to be mad at me for wanting you safe?" She searches my eyes for a brief moment before shaking her head. "Good," I whisper before tipping my head with every intention of claiming those lips of hers.

Just when I'm about to taste her, the cat jumps up on the counter and startles us. He looks at me with weary eyes before plopping his butt down into a sitting position. I don't know how to react around cats. Growing up, the only kind of animal we had was dogs, and all the cats that I've met before have all been temperamental.

I decide to test the waters and reach out my hand to pet him. "Hi, Apollo." He immediately swats at my arm, scratching me with his claws. I pull back to inspect the underside of my forearm and see a long red slash. I glare at the little fucker for getting me good; this shit stings.

"That's what you get for suggesting a dog in his house." Aly smirks at me while she grabs Apollo and takes him off of the counter. "You better start wooing him. If Apollo won't love you, then I don't know if I can."

I narrow my eyes at her and watch her expression to see if she's joking. *She better be fucking joking.* She can only manage a straight face for five seconds before a giggle finally escapes her. I grab her wrists and haul her against me then link her arms around my waist, bring my hands up to cup her cheeks and pull her face to mine. I start to kiss her softly, nibbling gently on her bottom lip while trying to remind myself to keep things slow and let her take the lead.

The minute her tongue touches my lips, I'm done being a gentleman. I growl loudly as I part my mouth, my hands plunging roughly into her hair, and I deepen our kiss. Every stroke of our tongues against each other has my dick hardening until it's painfully screaming to be let out. I break free of our kiss, resting my forehead against hers while we catch our breaths.

"I think it's time to go upstairs and go to sleep," I say in a husky voice. I look at my watch to see it's already past midnight, leaving me just a few hours before I have to head home to grab my suitcase that is already packed. "I need to be up in four hours so I can go back home to grab my shit."

"Are you sure you still want to spend the night? You would probably get more sleep if you went home." She looks at me with concern, and her thoughtfulness for my well-being warms my heart.

"I can sleep on the plane. You just need to behave and keep your hands to yourself tonight or we both won't be getting any sleep," I warn her with a joking smile and she laughs. I drop a kiss on her forehead, and she grabs my hand to lead me up the stairs to her bedroom.

The master suite takes up the whole second floor, with the second bedroom being downstairs off the kitchen. It's a huge room with vaulted ceilings, a ceiling fan, and two windows with a view of the backyard. Her bedroom is decorated in the same style and colors as the rest of the house - warm, cozy, and inviting.

"Did you bring anything else to wear to bed?" she inquires while glancing at my T-shirt and jeans.

"Considering I usually sleep naked, no, I didn't." Her eyes go wide and I laugh at her deer-in-headlights expression. "Don't worry, I'll sleep in my boxers tonight. If you really feel you have no self-control around me, I'll sleep fully clothed."

Her lips twitch and she rolls her eyes at me. "Sleeping in jeans is uncomfortable. I'm fine if you keep your boxers on." She walks past me to the bathroom and pulls out a basket from underneath the cabinet. "Here's an extra toothbrush, and you can borrow some of my toothpaste." She puts a new toothbrush down next to one of the sinks of the double vanity.

I watch her pull out toothpaste from a drawer, put some on her toothbrush, and start to brush her teeth. I follow her lead, and we stare at each other through the mirror the whole time until her electric toothbrush shuts off. I leave her to finish and go back in the bedroom. I take my shoes and socks off, followed by my shirt and jeans. The moment I pull back the comforter to get into bed, Aly's perfume drifts into the air, annihilating my senses.

I groan as my cock reacts and I try to hide myself underneath the sheets. I throw one arm over my eyes and tell myself to go to sleep. *Pretend you're in your grandma's house, Gavin. Trick your mind into thinking you aren't in Aly's bed, but your grandmother's old moth-ball-smelling guestroom.*

My mental mind game starts working until I hear the bathroom door open, the lights turn off, and the pitter-patter of her feet coming closer and closer to me. I feel the covers slide off me as she pulls them back, and the bed shifts under her weight. I wait to feel her lie down next to me, but after a couple of minutes, nothing happens. I peek out from underneath my arm to see her staring at my abdomen. Having her this close and watching me causes my dick to immediately stand at attention.

"Aly, you need to stop," I warn her as I take my other hand and try to cover myself.

"You have an eight-pack. How is that even possible?" She reaches out and starts counting my ab muscles, each stroke of her finger jolting my dick higher and higher until it's aching against my belly.

"Aly," I moan out in a plea. "Stop touching me and go to sleep!" Unable to trust myself if she keeps this up, I flop over onto my stomach, turn my head in the opposite direction, and grip my cock with my hands to keep it from going anywhere near her.

"Okay," she says reluctantly. I feel her lie down and get the covers settled over both of us. The silence only lasts for about one minute before she loudly sighs and starts fidgeting. I feel her flipping back and forth between her back and her stomach. Finally, she inches closer to me and wraps her arm around my back.

"Are you okay?" I twist my head to face her to find we're merely inches apart. I grit my teeth, telling myself to behave and not kiss her, because if I start, I won't be able to stop.

"Yeah, it's just been a long time since someone has slept in bed with me, so my body isn't used to it."

The thought of someone else besides me being in this bed with her makes me want to put my fucking fist through the wall. "Get used to it, darlin', because this is going to become a regular occurrence."

"I hope so," she whispers, her minty breath tickling my nose. She leans forward and places a soft kiss on my forehead. *Goddamn, this girl is one of the sweetest fucking people I've ever met.*

"Are you nervous about tomorrow night? I can't believe this is your first late-night show appearance." I feel her start to draw circles on my back, the mere touch of her fingers sending sparks down my spine to my toes. I have to blink a couple times to remember what she just asked me.

"No, I'm not nervous, but that'll be a different story once we're there. You know they do most of the taping of the shows in the afternoon and it's broadcast later that day, right?" She shakes her head and I continue on. "The daytime talk shows start taping at 12:30 pm, so as soon as we land, we'll go straight to our hotel to get styled and ready before performing on The Ellen Clarkson Show. Then it'll just be a whirlwind of more shows and interviews the whole time we're there."

"Is Sosie excited about the trip?"

"Sosie is actually not going. She prefers to never step foot in the state of California ever again," I tell her with a yawn, and I suddenly start to feel tired. My dick has finally deflated enough to where I can lie next to her and not be in pain anymore.

"Why is that?" she asks, and I hesitate a little. If Aly is going to be in my life the way I want her to be, then she needs to know everything. My gut is telling me I can trust that she won't tell Sosie I told her.

"Sosie left California to get away from her parents, because they're drug addicts. They've been that way for most of her life. When they lived in Austin, my parents tried to protect her anytime my aunt and uncle got in trouble with

AURORA ROSE REYNOLDS/JESSICA MARIN

the law. She lived with us during the times they were sent to jail or rehab, but they never stayed clean long. I think the longest they ever did was two years."

"Oh my God, that's awful! No wonder Sosie seems so hostile."

"Hostile is a nice way to put it." I chuckle, because Sosie can be a raging bitch sometimes for no reason other than the chip on her shoulder, and her distrust for everyone she doesn't personally know.

"When did they move to California?" Aly asks.

"When she was thirteen. Out of the blue, my uncle said they were moving, because he got a job out there. Never told my dad he was even considering leaving Austin. The main core of the family still lives in Austin, so it was a shock that anyone would want to leave." I'll never forget that day for as long as I live. Sosie was screaming and bawling her eyes out, begging my parents to please adopt her so she didn't have to go. We asked her parents if she could live with us, but they refused.

"Sosie hated California and being taken away from our family. I think deep down she knew her parents were on a downward spiral. Fortunately, she had wonderful neighbors who helped take care of her until she could take care of herself. We would talk every day and keep a countdown to the day she turned eighteen. Once she graduated high school, we bought her a one-way ticket back to Austin, and she moved in with my parents."

"Poor Sosie. That really makes me sad for her."

"Even being back home, Sosie felt on edge. She had this nagging feeling they would come back. When my schedule was getting too crazy for me to control, I offered her a job to be my assistant, and she's been here ever since." I sigh, hating the fact that my aunt and uncle are such scum to not give a fuck about their daughter. How Sosie didn't turn out to be like them is a miracle.

"I don't have any plans on Sunday. Do you think Sosie would want to hang out with me?" Aly asks in a tired, soft voice.

"You don't have to do that, baby." I bring my hand up to her cheek, my thumb caressing her cheekbone. *How is this gorgeous, amazing creature still single? And how am I the lucky bastard she's willing to take a chance on?*

"I know I don't have to, but I want to," Aly says before yawning. I slide my arm down her waist, cup her hip with my hand, and pull her against me.

"I'll give you her phone number before I leave. Promise me you won't be upset if she tells you no?" I ask her softly.

"I promise." Her voice is barely a whisper, and I know she's on the verge of sleep.

"Sweet dreams, baby." I kiss her lightly on the lips and listen to her breathing, a sound I realize I want to listen to every night for the rest of my life.

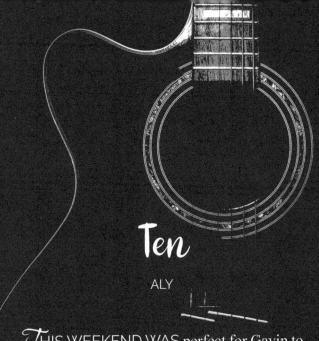

Ten

ALY

*T*HIS WEEKEND WAS perfect for Gavin to be out of town, because I had to work both Friday and Saturday evenings. Fortunately, my Sunday was free, and thank the Lord it is, because I feel like I got hit by a train, and alcohol wasn't even involved. My body is rebelling against me for the late nights of work and phone conversations with Gavin. Today has been the first day in a very long time that I slept past ten in the morning, and even then, I'm still exhausted. Normally, my Sundays are reserved for spending time with my family, but both my parents and Valerie are out of town, leaving all day to do whatever I want.

I roll over in my bed, grab the pillow Gavin slept on, and hug it to my body. I haven't had the heart to change my sheets since he was here, because his intoxicating scent still lingers on them. I press my nose into the pillow and smile, hoping he was serious when he said sleepovers will be a regular occurrence. It's crazy he's only slept over once and the bed feels empty without him.

How can I miss him so much when I just met him?

Despite my busy work schedule this weekend, I thought about him constantly. I didn't have to worry about whether or not he was missing me, because he's called and texted numerous times proving without words he's in as deep as me. Even when he's not around, he still knows how to melt my heart with grandiose gestures. Flowers from him were delivered to my office Friday morning, but the biggest surprise came from what he said during his interview on The Ellen Clarkson Show.

I warned Gavin when he left my house that morning that I would have to record both of his televised performances, since they were airing during times I was working and I wouldn't be able to watch them until right before I went to bed. So when my phone started ringing off the hook Friday afternoon, I didn't think much of it. The first call was from Willow, but I ignored it, because I was at a music video shoot for one of my clients. But when my boss called, I stepped outside to pick up, hoping there weren't any emergencies.

"Holy balls, it's world official!" Shane screamed in excitement into the phone, his voice going a mile a minute. "Are you on cloud nine? Are you happy? Scared? Knowing you, you're probably freaking out. I'm freaking out for you! *Ahhh!*"

"Whoa, slow down, Shane! Or you'll be banned from any kind of caffeine for the rest of the day," I told him, feeling like a mom banning candy from her toddler. "I can't even understand you, you're talking so fast. What in the world is going on?"

"Are you serious right now? Do you really not know?" he questioned at first and then started to laugh hysterically. "Oh, this is classic. Where are you right now?"

"You should know. You're my boss!" I told him sarcastically, not understanding what in the hell was going on with him.

"Aly, do you honestly think I can keep up with all my minions? I can't remember what I even did yesterday, let alone know everyone's work schedule."

I didn't have a response to that, since he did have a point. "I'm at Skylar Ryan's music video shoot."

"Why didn't you take a break to go watch Gavin's interview on The Ellen Clarkson show?"

"Because I'm going to watch it later tonight."

"Does he know that?"

I roll my eyes. "Yes, I told him I'd record it and watch it when I get home this evening."

"Go home right now and watch it," he demanded, shocking me with this request. "And you're not allowed to take phone calls from anyone else until you've seen it. Even if Gavin is calling you, do not pick up."

"Is he okay? Did something happen?" My heart started to pound at the thought of something bad happening to Gavin.

"Oh, he's more than okay. Leave now, Aly. Everyone will be fine without you for an hour."

"Shane, it's unprofessional for me to leave in the middle of a shoot. I can just watch it later—"

"Aly," he cut me off. "As your boss, I'm telling you to go home. That's an order!" he said fiercely into the phone. "I don't care if you skip his whole performance as long as you watch the interview." Shane giggled like a lunatic, and I was seriously wondering if he was on something other than caffeine.

"Fine, I'll leave now and call you when I'm done."

"Don't forget to call me." He hung up before I could, and I didn't know what he was on, but my curiosity was peaked.

Fortunately, my house was close to where the music video shoot was, and it took me no time at all to get back home. I ran inside the house, turned on the TV, and went through my recordings to find the show. I didn't skip over Gavin's performance like Shane suggested. I wanted to watch him in his element, and even through the television, I was mesmerized by those green eyes and that deep voice. I fast-forwarded through the commercials and stopped when the show was back on. Gavin looked his normal, hot self, wearing a blue-and-orange plaid button-down shirt that clung to his chest and biceps, dark denim jeans, and black leather high-tops. Ellen was congratulating him on the success of "User" and listed out all the songs he had written for other artists. She genuinely seemed impressed as she read off the titles and artists of the songs, and I can admit I was impressed too.

"Now, Gavin, I have to ask the burning question the ladies in my audience are dying to know," Ellen said to him, and the crowd started applauding as if they already knew what she was going to ask. "Is Gavin McNeer single? And if so, where would we find him mingling?"

Gavin laughed, and my heart felt like it was beating out of my chest from the anticipation of his answer.

"No, I'm not single. I'm very much taken by a beautiful woman named Alyson."

As soon as he said that, I paused the recording and studied his happy expression while my heart seemed to explode in my chest.

Even two days later, I still can't believe it. When we talked later that night, he asked if I was upset with him, and of course, I told him no. How could I be upset with him? He just told the whole world we're dating. If that doesn't prove he's committed to us, then I don't know what else would.

A marriage proposal would.

Don't even go there, brain!

I shake my head at myself and wonder why I would even think such a silly thought. *We just met less than a week ago!* I still need to figure out how to navigate my relationship with him. In all honesty, I don't know how to feel about the news of us being together made public. While it makes me feel amazing to know he wants to be with me, the fact that people want to know all about me just because I'm dating him is scary. Someone even reported my last name to a news source, and my Facebook and Instagram pages blew up with likes and messages. Most have been sweet, but some have been pretty nasty, with people telling me I wasn't good enough for Gavin, a few even threatening me to stay away from him or else.

After the last threat I received, I shut down

both my accounts, since I don't really need to have social media anyway. Fans can be crazy, and they are easy to ignore, but the people I work with starting to look at me differently is a little harder to deal with. Before his appearance on television, my co-workers started to ask if Gavin and I were dating, and I was hesitant in answering them, wanting to keep whatever we were starting private for as long as possible. Now, I can't do that anymore.

Don't worry about the unknown, Aly, I tell myself, *what's meant to be, will be.* I'm just going to be grateful that such a wonderful man like Gavin is even interested in me. He's sneaking his way into my heart and I know I'll be devastated if he decides I'm not worth his time anymore. *Get those thoughts out of your head!* Gavin has made it clear he wants to be with me and I want to be with him, so no more hesitations. Time to enjoy every minute I have with him.

On that note, I get up out of bed and decide a little retail therapy and a movie would do me good. I fix myself some toast with peanut butter on it, brew some coffee, and give Apollo some love before feeding him. Once I'm done with breakfast, I get dressed, and just as I'm about to leave, I remember I was going to call Sosie and invite her out with me. Sosie is important to Gavin, and I really want the two of us to try to become friends. I sit down on my couch, take a deep breath, and dial her number.

"Hello?" she answers, and even in greeting, she sounds pissed off and annoyed.

"Hey, Sosie, it's Aly. How are you?" I ask cheerfully, hoping that maybe if she hears my good mood, she'll be nice.

"How did you get my number?" she asks with irritation, not even bothering to answer my question or, out of politeness, ask how I am.

"I asked Gavin for your number before he left. I was working all weekend but have today free and was hoping we could hang out."

"Hang out?" she repeats as if she doesn't understand what that even means.

"Yeah, hang out. Want to meet me for a movie? I haven't been to one in a long time and thought it would be fun if we could go and get to know each other better."

"Why would I want to get to know you better?"

"Well." Her rudeness stumps me, and I'm momentarily left speechless. I pull myself together and use the skills I have when dealing with artists. "Don't you think it would be nice to be friends for Gavin's sake, especially since I'm dating him and we're going to be seeing a lot more of each other?"

"I have enough friends, Alyson, so my friendship quota is full. Not to mention, I'm not interested in being your friend. Furthermore, I would like to go on the record and say that if you hurt my cousin, I'll blacklist you from ever working at any record label ever again."

I snort at her threat, knowing full well she doesn't have that kind of power. *What a bitch!*

"If anyone's going to get hurt from this relationship, it will end up being me," I respond with a cold voice. "I would never hurt or betray your cousin. I'm not Tori." Bile rises in my throat at the thought of being compared to that woman. I understand Sosie is just trying to protect Gavin, but she needs to give people a chance before making judgement.

"Gavin's never been the type of guy to cheat on anyone. If he wasn't interested, you'd be gone already." She sighs in frustration.

"You barely know him. Let's not get ahead of ourselves here."

"You're right, Sosie. I barely know him, but from what I've seen so far, he's a damn fine man and I don't plan on letting him slip away." I drag in a breath. "So, let's act like adults and be cordial and respectful to one another. There's no need to be rude to me. We both have his best interests at heart."

"*I* have his best interests at heart. The verdict is still out on you," she snaps, and I gasp at her words, anger making me stand up from my couch. "Don't call me again unless it's an emergency." And with that, she hangs up on me.

I stare at my phone in shock, enraged that she not only spoke to me the way she did, but she also hung up on me. I throw my phone down on the couch and scream out in frustration. Never have I had someone talk to me the way she just did. I start to pace, wondering how I should handle this situation. Should I tell Gavin, so he understands why there will be tension between the two of us?

No, I shouldn't. I don't want to be the cause of his relationship with Sosie to diminish.

Family comes first for a lot of people, and in no way would I be the one to put him in a position where he would have to choose between me and her. Sosie seems to be the type who would pressure Gavin to make a choice between us if things got bad, and I'm not one hundred percent confident yet that he would even choose me.

I decide it isn't worth telling him right now. All I can do is prove to Sosie that I'm here to stay and want Gavin for the right reasons.

Eleven

GAVIN

I LOOK OUT the window of the plane in eagerness, the landscape of western Tennessee twenty thousand feet below, indicating we're almost home. Dawn is approaching, with orange, lavender, and pink starting to light the sky, the promise of a beautiful day imminent. I decided to change my flight home and was able to catch the last seat on the red eye back to Nashville. I've barely slept, my excitement at seeing Aly and surprising her keeping me awake.

With so much adrenaline coursing through me, I was able to work on Patty's song and start writing another one for myself, with Aly as my muse. I haven't shared with her yet that she's been my inspiration while writing my next album. I'm waiting until one of the songs is fully mastered and then I'll surprise her with it. Hopefully, she'll love it.

I sit back and reflect on how amazing my trip to Los Angeles was. All our performances went without a hitch, and I made some new contacts that can only help me in the future. It was a successful trip out west, and hopefully I can bring Aly with me the next time I go. I look at my watch to see it's 5:30 in the morning. I purposely kept my calendar open for today, and we should land with just enough time for me to take her out to breakfast.

Our descent into Nashville goes quickly, and within thirty minutes, we land smoothly. Sitting up in first class provides me the opportunity to get off the plane within minutes of arriving at the gate. I walk hastily through the airport, down to baggage claim, where I wait for my luggage and guitar. Once those are retrieved, I grab an Uber and head to Aly's house.

Traffic is still relatively light at this time in

the morning, so we arrive at her house much earlier than I anticipated. As soon as the Uber leaves, I question if she's even up yet for work. In my haste to see her, I didn't think things through. Now I wonder if I should call another Uber to come get me and take me home. I can drop off my stuff and then drive back here to get her.

Fuck that! I want to see her, and if that means waking her up, then so be it.

I walk up to her door and press the doorbell, making sure I'm in the camera's line of sight so she can see it's me. Thirty seconds go by, and I start to think she might still be sleeping, when the door is pulled open and she stands there in front of me, her eyes wide in surprise.

"You're here," she whispers, but I can't seem to form any words as my eyes drink in her wet hair plastered to her head, a long, white fluffy robe tied tightly around her body, and her cute bare feet with light-pink-painted toenails peeking out from the bottom. Aly was in the shower, meaning she's gloriously naked underneath that robe.

Fuck me.

I don't think, just react. I barge right into

her house, forcing her to take a couple steps back, drop my belongings, and grab her. She reaches up for me at the same time and fuses our lips together, her hunger for me just as strong as mine is for her. We both moan out loud every time our tongues touch, relishing in the pleasure of being back in each other's arms. Our kisses are raw and sensual but with a hint of desperation, as we're both searching for more.

"Goddamn, I missed you," I growl before capturing her mouth and plunging my tongue between her lips. I kick the door shut so no one can see us and lift her up, her legs automatically going around my waist. She gasps as my hand squeezes her ass and positions her against my raging hard-on. She breaks our kiss and pulls back, staring at me while she catches her breath.

"How are you here right now? I thought your plane wasn't supposed to get in until this afternoon."

"I took the red eye home. I wanted to surprise you," I say while my lips make a trail of wet kisses down her neck. I kiss across her sternum, tasting her rose-flavored soap, and I crave to taste more. I've never been so turned on by the mere touch of a woman before her.

"This is the best surprise ever," she whispers as she pulls my head back up for another scorching kiss.

I hold onto her and walk us to the nearest bedroom, consumed with the need to taste her. I gently lay her down and stand back to look at her sprawled out before me. The sash to her robe is barely tied, giving me a glimpse of the valley in between her breasts. My hands shake as I reach for the knot and slowly pull on one of the strings. She watches me the whole time, her eyes hooded in desire. Once the knot is undone, I pull back the robe and suck in my breath at the beauty that is her body.

"My God, you're exquisite," I marvel as I plant my knee against the bed, bend down so my right arm is supporting my weight, and reach out with my other hand to caress her left breast. Her flesh fills the palm of my hand perfectly, her nipples and areoles a beautiful shade of blush. I watch, mesmerized as her nipple perks up between my fingers, my mouth salivating to taste it.

Unable to wait any longer, I lean down

and take the delicate bud into my mouth. She arches her back and moans, her fingers threading through my hair and tugging my head closer to her. I continue to flick my tongue over her nipple, enjoying the purr of her moans and the taste of her skin. I kiss my way over to her other breast, making sure it gets equal attention.

"Do you like me sucking on your tits, baby?" She hesitantly nods. "Are your nipples too sensitive for this?" I graze my teeth lightly against one, her body springing up from the touch.

"No," she mewls, her noises driving me fucking insane with desire. Her nails scratch against my scalp, sending shivers down my spine as I continue my assault on her breasts. I feel her rubbing her pussy against my cock, and it takes all my willpower not to grab it out of my jeans and plunge right into her.

Fuck, I need to be inside her, but I want her in control of when that happens. I don't want her ever having doubts that she's just a fling for me. She's made a permanent mark on my heart and has the power to completely destroy it. Her hold over me in such a short amount of time is more powerful than any other woman I've had in my life. I can tell she only wants me for me and not Gavin McNeer, the celebrity. Knowing how much I needed to see her again only confirmed this girl is going to be mine. But until she says she's ready for me to take her, I'll give her the next best thing.

I take one last hard pull of her nipple and start kissing my way down her abdomen, zigzagging my way across her curves until I get to the top of her mound. Her legs automatically part for me, and I take that as permission to continue my journey down south. I get on my knees and trace my finger over her clit, lifting my eyes off what my fingers are doing. I watch her watch me, and I almost come undone when she bites her bottom lip and moans as I insert my finger inside her. Her slick, wet pussy pulsates around my finger and I groan, closing my eyes and imagining sinking inside her.

"Darlin', I'm struggling here. I need to taste you, but I need to know you're okay with that." My voice is gruff, the pleasure of just my finger inside her so intense that I can't even let my mind wonder to what it's going to be like once I'm finally inside her.

"Yes, please yes," she cries out while my finger continues to go in and out, over her clit, and back in. Without wasting any time, I quickly replace my finger with my tongue, burying myself in her. I use my hands on her inner thighs to open her wider, sucking and licking as much of her as I can. God-fucking-damn, she tastes like heaven, and I continue licking, sucking, biting, never wanting this to end.

"Gavin," she murmurs, her head thrashing from side to side on the covers. "Please." I know what she's begging for, and I'm more than ready to give it to her. I slowly insert two fingers and start their back and forth rhythm. Soon, her hips are bucking wildly against me, and I increase the speed of my fingers. Her sweet, juicy syrup is spilling all over me, and I can't lap it up fast enough. The taste of her, the feel of her, has got me so hard I don't give a fuck if I come all over myself.

"Oh my God... Gavin... I'm going to come," she gasps and tugs my hair harder. I can feel her walls repeatedly clenching around me, and I know she's almost there. I suck harder on her clit while my fingers fuck her deeper.

"Come, baby. Don't hold back," I tell her as she starts grinding against my face and fingers.

She screams out my name, grabs my head, and clenches me against her as hard as she can, her walls completely holding my fingers hostage as she seizes up and comes. I lift my head and watch her slowly come down from her intense orgasm. The look of pure bliss on her face is one I want to memorize. Her legs slump down and I slowly ease my fingers out of her.

"Fuck, baby, you tasted better than I even imagined you would," I murmur against her stomach as I continue kissing my way up her body. "I plan on eating you forever."

"Oh my God, my body is tingling right now," she whispers, pushing my head away from her body while it continues spasming. "I don't think my body could handle you doing that forever." She smiles, running her fingers through my hair as she leans up to touch her mouth to mine. "But I really wouldn't mind it on occasion. Okay, maybe more than that."

I chuckle at her statement and decide to give

AURORA ROSE REYNOLDS/JESSICA MARIN

her some space by using the restroom. "I'll be back." I stand up and wince from the pain of my erection, walking to the guest bathroom. Once inside, I close the door, turn on the sink, and splash my face with cold water, hoping the shock of it will calm my dick down. I dry my face off and take a couple deep breaths.

Aly is going to be the death of me.

I shake my head at myself and open the door to see she's not lying on the bed anymore. I walk out into the living room and figure she's getting ready for work when I hear her blow dryer click on. I make us some coffee and check my text messages while it brews. Once it's done, I pour myself and her each a cup and bring hers to her.

Our eyes lock in the mirror, and she smiles shyly at me, heat flushing her cheeks. That dimple I'm starting to love pops out, and I decide to kiss her cheek exactly where it is. I sit down on the closed lid of the toilet and drink my coffee, enjoying my view as I watch her get ready.

"Are you really going to sit there and watch me get ready for work?" she asks.

"Yeah." I shrug one shoulder, not really

having a response. I just want to be around her all the time. She shakes her head with a slight smile on her face.

"Suit yourself," she mumbles before continuing to put on her makeup.

We sit there in comfortable silence while I watch her get ready, and I see she's struggling not to laugh as she continues avoiding me to concentrate on her makeup. I could stare at her all day and all night long; she's that fucking gorgeous. I take a sip of my coffee and decide to break the silence.

"I realized this weekend that I haven't taken you out on a formal date yet."

"You've taken me out to breakfast, and we've had dinner. Those to me are all dates, so you have nothing to apologize for."

"I don't consider those 'real' dates. I want to take you out to a nice dinner."

She rolls her eyes at me, and if she weren't holding that mascara wand close to her eye, I would spank her ass for her sassiness.

"I don't need to be taken out to nice dinners. I'm good with any kind of alone time I can get with you." She turns to smile at me seductively before she goes back to concentrating on what she's doing. My gaze rakes down her body and my cock starts twitching at the thought of bending her over that counter, pulling up that sundress of hers that she's now wearing, and fucking her from behind. I must have groaned out loud, because she stops applying her makeup and looks over at me in concern.

"You okay?" she asks, turning to look at me briefly.

"Never better." I wink and silently will my dick to calm the fuck down.

Think of moth balls and grandmas, Gavin.

"Back to the topic of dinner." I clear my throat and gulp down the pain in my groin. "Do you have to work tonight? Because if not, I'm taking you out."

She thinks for a moment before responding. "I think I'm free tonight."

"Excellent. I'll pick you up at seven."

She smiles and gives me that adorable, sexy smirk again, and I seriously contemplate the idea of leaving now so I can go home and jerk off to the memories of what I just did to her.

She continues glancing at me in between putting her makeup away before finally closing her drawer and turning to me, crossing her arms over her chest. "You know, you got out of bed kind of quickly this morning. I really wanted to make you come by sucking you off, but I guess you weren't interested."

I spit my coffee out all over her wall and start coughing. She hands me a towel and pounds on my back, laughing the whole time.

"Arms up, Gavin. It will help you breathe." She walks in front of me and holds my arms up, my line of vision directly in front of her marvelous breasts.

Once the coughing subsides, she lets go of my arms, and I quickly snake them around her waist and bring her down on top of me. "Don't ever say that to me while I'm drinking hot beverages, and I'm always interested in you sucking me off." I lift my head and kiss her, loving the fact that my girl looks sweet and innocent on the outside but has a dirty mouth in the bedroom. I can't wait for her to become one hundred percent comfortable with me to find out just how dirty she can get.

"How about a raincheck for tonight then?" she moans out as I grind her hips against my cock so she can feel exactly what she does to me. I plunge my tongue through her parted lips, needing to get my fill of her one more time before I stop this so she can go to work.

"It's a date," I tell her as I break our kiss and stare into her eyes, trying to regain some sense of my sanity back. She plants one more soft kiss on my lips before standing up and leaving my lap. I watch her ass as she walks out of the bathroom before I breathe in deep and exhale out a shaky breath. I look up at the ceiling and pray for endurance that I don't come in her mouth after two licks from that wicked tongue of hers tonight.

Please, Lord, let this girl be the one, I add silently to my prayers. As fucking crazy as it sounds, I'm falling hard and fast for Alyson Dawson, and I know there's no turning back.

Twelve

$\mathcal{A}$LL DAY LONG, I've had a permanent smile on my face just thinking about Gavin and what's in store for us tonight. The day seemed to drag by, and I could barely focus at work, which has never happened before. When it was time for me to leave the office, my excitement turned to nervous energy, making me anxious to get home to find the perfect outfit. Earlier, I texted Gavin to find out where he's taking me and what the dress code is, but his response back was vague, only telling me to wear a dress.

I wash my face to reapply my makeup, this

time going with a heavier, smoky eye look and light lipstick. I curl my long hair into soft waves and then pin a small section of it above my right ear with a bedazzled bobby pin. I decided on a tight, black, off-the-shoulder, long-sleeved dress that stops right above my knees, with strappy black, high heel sandals and sparkling jewelry at my ears and neck. The doorbell rings just as I'm checking myself out in the mirror, and I pray that Gavin likes what he sees.

My answer comes quickly when I open the door and Gavin's eyes widen, his gaze slowly trailing down my body and back up again to meet my eyes. I'm starting to recognize this intense gaze of his means he's turned on and thinking of doing very naughty things to me.

I love that look coming from him.

"Goddamn, darlin'." He takes a deep breath and closes his eyes as if he's in pain.

I grab his wrist and pull him inside then open my mouth to ask him what's wrong, since I've never seen him look like he does right now. Just when the words start to leave my mouth, my mind goes in a completely different direction and my breath catches. I've never seen him look hotter. He looks ruggedly handsome, wearing a charcoal gray sports coat with matching slacks, a black belt around his narrow hips, and a white button-down shirt that shows off just how in shape he is. "Wow," I murmur, as my eyes do another once-over. "You look incredible."

He opens his eyes, swallows, and then looks at me as he groans out, "It hurts to not be inside you. It's taking every ounce of willpower I have to not pick you up, hike up that damn dress, and have you ridin' me so hard that this whole neighborhood hears you screaming my name when you come."

My eyes widen as he stares at me with unabashed desire. I blink.

Damn, there went my panties.

"It's fine, darlin'. I can wait until after dinner to make you my dessert for tonight." He gives me a devilish smile, and I'm ready for him to have me for dessert now.

Screw dinner!

"Will you excuse me for a second? I forgot something upstairs. Be right back," I say quickly in a high, squeaky voice. I run back upstairs, when an idea comes to me. One I've never had before.

Do it! Just do it, my mind screams.

The idea is scary and exhilarating all at the same time. I pull off my thong and throw it in the hamper. I turn on all the lamps in my room and look closely at myself in the mirror, hoping it's not too obvious I'm not wearing anything underneath.

"Aly, you okay up there?" I hear Gavin ask from the bottom of the stairs.

I jump, startled from his voice. "Coming!" I yell and hear him mumble something I can't understand. I shut off all the lights and go back downstairs. The sensation of wearing no underwear beneath my dress is foreign, and I take the stairs slower than normal.

"You ready to go?" he asks, and I nod, grabbing my purse, and we leave the house. Gavin reaches for my hand after I lock the front door and leads me down my front yard pathway. I look around for his truck but become confused when he walks straight to a car I've never seen before.

"Whoa, this is fancy. Whose car is this?" I give him a quizzical look when he opens the passenger door to a silver Tesla Model S. All

I've ever seen him drive is his truck, but then again, if this is his car, it's just a reminder of how we barely know each other.

"This is my newborn baby Sheila." I laugh as he accentuates his accent when calling the car Sheila. "You are her first female passenger. Even Sosie hasn't had a test drive yet."

I thank him for opening the door and step in, holding my dress down so it doesn't ride up and flash him my surprise. He closes my door and runs around the front of the car to the driver's side. I look around and admire the sleek interior of the car with minimalistic features and a huge touchscreen running down the middle console. I watch Gavin sink inside his seat and close the door. My man looks very sexy driving his luxury car, and I immediately have to press my legs together to quench the spark that radiates up my core.

"How long have you had baby Sheila?" I inquire, knowing these cars are very expensive.

"Just a couple months. When 'Thief of My Heart' went platinum, I decided to treat myself."

"You deserve it. The song is amazing." Despite my dislike for Tori, I can admit she does add something beautiful to that song, even though I know he was the mastermind behind the production and writing of it.

He grabs my hand and kisses my knuckles, his warm lips branding my skin. "Thank you, darlin'. That really means a lot coming from you."

He tells me I'm in charge of the music, so I find a playlist of '80s hair bands to torture him with. To my surprise, he actually likes some of the songs and sings along. I'm learning that even though Gavin prefers to sing country music, his musical tastes are just as eclectic as mine are.

Our drive is short, and we pull into the valet parking of one of the ritzier hotels in downtown Nashville. Once we leave the car, Gavin grabs my hand and we walk into the hotel to take the elevators up to the rooftop restaurant. The doors slide open, and as soon as the hostess sees Gavin, she hands our menus to another hostess, who escorts us to our table.

The restaurant is beautiful with windows all around for a 360-degree view of Nashville at night. The hostess drops us off at one of the tables by the windows. We sit down, and while the nighttime view is magnificent, I can only imagine how breathtaking it is during the day. She hands us our menus and tells us our waiter will be with us shortly. We thank her and open our menus, and my eyebrows shoot up in surprise at the prices. Even though I knew by the looks of the restaurant that it was expensive, I wasn't expecting it to be *this* expensive.

"Is the menu okay for you? I didn't even ask if you eat steak," Gavin questions while studying me intently, his menu already closed and put down on the edge of the table.

"The menu is fine, thank you." I lean in closer to him across the table. "You know I don't need fancy restaurants, right? I'm pretty laid back when it comes to food." I'm such a homebody that sometimes I will take a bowl of cereal over going out to a restaurant.

"Darlin', I know you don't, but if I want to take you out to fancy restaurants, please let me." He reaches his hand out, and I place mine in his, loving how well our hands fit together. "Okay?" He raises his eyebrow at me, a sexy smirk playing on his lips, and I know the topic is over.

"Okay." I sigh with a smile back at him. I get lost staring into those eyes and want to pinch myself, still not believing this is real. That this amazingly kind, hot-as-sin man is sitting here across from me and wants to be my boyfriend. *Me*. I don't know what I did to deserve this, but I will never take him or our relationship for granted.

"What's going on in that pretty little head of yours, baby? There are various emotions playing out all over your face." He smiles gently at me and he reaches underneath the table to caress my knee. His touch distracts me, making me momentarily forget the question he just asked.

"All I'm thinking about is how hot you look tonight and how very, very grateful I am to be here with you." I decide to be honest with him, because I need him to know my hesitation about us is slowly diminishing. My instincts are screaming at me to trust him, to take this leap of faith with him despite my uncomfortableness with his fame and all of the scrutiny that comes with it. I feel if I let all my doubts and worries go, then something beautiful is going to come out of this.

Something beautiful that just might last forever.

He looks around and leans in closer, his hand sliding up my thigh. "Baby, if you keep looking at me that way, we're not going to make it through dinner."

I give him a sexy smile and lean in as well, my hand strategically placed on his inner thigh. "Just to warn you, if your hand keeps traveling any farther north, it will discover that there is no barrier stopping you from touching me."

His smile falters, an intense hunger shining from his eyes. I gasp when he squeezes my thigh, his fingers on my bare skin making me wet all over again. If it wasn't for the table in between us and the absence of a tablecloth, I have no doubt that Gavin would finger me right here, right now, in front of everyone.

The waitress arrives and breaks our spell. We both lean back into our seats and tell her what we want for dinner, although my appetite is not for food any longer. When she leaves, another waiter arrives with a bottle of champagne. I look at Gavin in surprise, wondering when he ordered this. The waiter pops the cork, pours the bubbly in the flutes, and hands them to us before leaving.

"Are we toasting to your successful trip to Los Angeles?" I ask, excited to toast to him and his continued success.

"No, darlin', we're toasting to the future of us." He holds up his flute and I follow his lead. "And we're toasting to the record labels on Music Row. If it weren't for them, we would've never met at the Bluebird Cafe." We clink our glasses together and watch each other sip our champagne. So engulfed are we in each other that we don't see someone approaching our table.

"Gavin, is this your cute little niece from Austin?" a high-pitched voice interrupts us, and I turn my head to see none other than Tori Langston standing at the edge of our table. I almost spit out my champagne but manage to gulp it down without choking.

She stands next to Gavin, her hand settling on his shoulder as she checks me out. I ignore the animalistic anger that takes over me at seeing her touching my man. She's wearing a very low-cut, long-sleeved, red silk jumper that shows off her ginormous fake breasts. A black belt cinches her tiny waist, accentuating the curves of her hips. She's a beautiful woman with her jet-black hair, striking blue eyes, high cheekbones, and filled in lips. I can see from the outside why Gavin was attracted to her, but I'm a little surprised how they managed to date for as long as they did without her true colors coming out sooner. Maybe Gavin was just blind to it or maybe she's just that good of an actress.

"You know damn well this isn't my niece," Gavin grits out while grabbing her wrist to remove her hand from his body. His grip on my hand tightens and his whole body becomes stiff, like he's ready to chase me if I run. All the warmth I saw seconds ago in his eyes has been replaced with malice, and he doesn't even try to hide his hatred for her.

"Well, aren't you going to introduce us then?" Tori's laugh is filled with fakeness, the sound of it causing Gavin's jaw to clench in anger.

"This is my girlfriend, Alyson. Now that introductions are made, let me ask you to kindly stay the fuck away from us." There's a dangerous tone to his voice, and I can tell he's having trouble keeping his cool.

AURORA ROSE REYNOLDS/JESSICA MARIN

"Gavin," I softly warn, squeezing his hand for comfort. While I know he doesn't want to give her the time of day, I don't want him making her mad enough to lash out and jeopardize his career. Yes, he's made a name for himself as a songwriter and most people in this town know how psycho she is, but she's still the daughter of one of the most powerful men in Nashville.

She continues with her boisterous laughter, acting as if Gavin said the funniest thing in the world. "Oh, Gavin, come on now. I thought we were letting bygones be bygones. And besides, I can't just stay away if we're nominated for an award together." She turns her attention back to me and asks, "Will you be there at the award nominees' luncheon next week?"

I feel Gavin squeeze my hand and I look at him, a silent apology for not telling me blaring from his eyes. I know the nominees were announced before we met, and I remember hearing "Thief of My Heart" was nominated for Song of the Year. I don't know why he hasn't mentioned it to me. Maybe he assumed I would be there for work. I refuse to let her see she's put doubt into my head as to why he hasn't invited me to attend with him.

I put on my poker face and smile coldly at her. "Of course I'll be there." I hold her stare, hoping she's reading loud and clear that she will not intimidate me.

"Great," she says with insincere enthusiasm. "I'll see you both next week then! Nice to meet you, Alicia. See ya around, Gavin." She gives a wink before turning on her heel and walking toward a group of people across the restaurant.

I shake my head at her immaturity of calling me a different name. I know she's only doing it to get a rise out of me, but that petty behavior does nothing but make me pity her for being such a bitch.

"Aly, I'm so sorry. I completely forgot about the luncheon," Gavin says as soon as Tori is out of earshot. His eyes search mine, trying to make sure I'm not upset.

"I figured as much, and it's all right; you have nothing to apologize for." I smile at him, trying to downplay the situation.

"You do know you have no choice but to attend with me, right?"

"Do you really want me to attend or are you saying that because of what just happened?" I hate that I even have to ask, but I can't help the tiny voice in my head questioning if he's just now saying he wants me to go out of guilt.

"Of course I want you with me. Fuck, if I could, I'd handcuff you to my side... so please get that look off your face and get rid of any doubts that she may have put in your head." His words wash away the doubt I was feeling. "It was an honest mistake not mentioning it to you."

"I believe you." I move forward and once again position my hand on his thigh underneath the table. We gaze at one another without saying a word, and suddenly, I feel a shift in the air between us. My body starts buzzing underneath the sensual heat of his stare, and I wish we were alone and not surrounded by so many people.

"How do you feel about getting out of here and taking our food to go?" he questions, making me wonder if he can now read my thoughts.

"I like that idea a lot." As soon as the words leave my mouth, he signals for our waitress and makes the request for our food to go and the check. The waitress comes back with both at the same time. Gavin throws down a couple hundred-dollar bills, grabs our food with one hand and my hand with his other, and we walk out of the restaurant. I ignore the stares from people in the elevator on our way down, and when the doors open, I sigh in relief to see that his car is parked right in front of the valet stand. Gavin opens my door for me to make sure I get in okay then puts our food in his trunk before he tips the valet guy and gets in behind the wheel.

The car ride to my house is silent, and I notice Gavin has a feral look in his eyes that is electrifying the energy inside the car. We come to a stoplight, and he rests his hand on my left thigh. I suck in my breath as his fingers start slowly trailing inward and down, getting lost inside my dress until I feel him touch my clit. I sink lower into my seat and spread my legs a little to give him easier access. He rests his palm on top of my mound and his fingers start to work their magic.

"Christ, I've been thinking about how wet you get ever since you told me you had no panties on underneath that sexy little dress of yours."

I moan out loud and close my eyes as wave after wave of pleasure starts rolling through my body. Wanting him to feel the same overwhelming desire I'm feeling, I reach out with my left hand and start touching him through his pants. I feel his cock pulse against my palm, making my walls clench with the need to have him inside me. While he continues to finger me, I pull down his zipper and reach in to grab him.

"Fuck, baby," he hisses as my hand reaches inside his boxers and wraps around his length. I gently squeeze then roll my hand upward and caress the rim underneath the head. I feel his precum start to drip into my palm, and I spread it around his tip and go down to the base again.

"Aly," he breathes, he eyes squinting as he tries to focus on the road. "You're going to make me crash the car if I come in your hand." I look around in a haze to try to figure out where we are and am happy to see we're almost to my house.

"I'm not stopping unless you stop." I gasp louder as he plunges his finger deeper inside me. My walls squeeze around him, and I can't stop my hips from gyrating against his hand. I can feel the pressure of my release building inside me, making my hand on his cock increase in tempo to match my hips.

"We're almost there," he growls out, and I don't know if he's talking about being close to my house or him close to coming, because I know I'm just a couple strokes away from ecstasy.

"Harder, Gavin," I pant, my need for my orgasm too great to stop now. He applies more pressure and starts rubbing me harder. As soon as he pulls into my driveway, I scream out to God and feel the explosion of my release rock through me. He pulls his finger out and I slump into my seat, my body shaking from the aftershocks of my orgasm.

"That was the hottest fucking thing I've ever seen in my life," Gavin whispers, and before I can react, he cups the back of my neck and brings my mouth to his. His kiss is all heat and desperation when his tongue passes between my parted lips. My hand rubs his cock faster, his hitched breathing indicating he's close to coming.

"Let's get inside," he demands in between

kisses. He wraps his fingers around my wrist to remove my hand from his dick. I don't argue, as I prefer we take things to my bedroom. We both push open our doors and get out. Gavin grabs the food out of the trunk, shuts it, and places his hand on the small of my back. His touch is gentle but forceful, since he's just as eager as I am to get inside the house and continue where we left off. I fumble getting my keys out of my purse, my hands shaking from so much anticipation. I finally get a hold of myself and am able to unlock the door.

"Go upstairs. I'll put the food away," Gavin says in a low, commanding voice while he shuts and locks my front door.

I do as he says without responding, my heels banging loudly against the stairs as I make my way up. I turn on the lamp next to my bed and sit down to take my sandals off. Just as I finish pulling off the last shoe, I look up to see Gavin standing in my doorway, watching me. I stand up and walk around to stand at the edge of the bed, waiting for him to come join me. He walks slowly, like a predator hunting his prey, and I know I'm going to give myself to him tonight.

He stops in front of me, his eyes holding me captive. I know he's searching for some sort of hesitation or doubt, but he's not going to find any. I noticed he took his coat and shoes off while downstairs. *Good, less clothing to remove.* My hands reach up and start unbuttoning his dress shirt. He stares at me the whole time, and when the last button is free, I pull back his shirt and move it down past his arms to reveal his sculpted chest and torso.

I drop the shirt to the floor and start planting soft kisses across his chest until my mouth lands on his nipple. His hands leave my waist and travel up into my hair, his deep moans indicating he's enjoying my mouth on him. While I continue giving each of his nipples some attention, my hands reach down and start to unbuckle his belt. I don't even bother removing it from his pants when I unbutton his trousers and stick my hand down the front of his boxers, taking hold of his erection.

"Baby," he groans and pulls me in for another scorching, delicious kiss. While our tongues tango together, I push his pants and underwear down his hips. Once his clothing is out of the way, I wrap my hand around his cock while my other one snakes around and squeezes his ass. He breaks away from our kiss, and I watch him close his eyes and shudder, an intoxicating power coming over me knowing I'm making him feel this way.

"Fuck, I'm not going to last long if you keep this up," he whispers as he presses his forehead against mine. "It's been a really long time."

This news surprises me, but I'm secretly ecstatic, because it's been a long time for me too. Stilling my hand, he steps back and kicks off his pants while I take the time to gaze at that incredible eight-pack and those hot-as-hell V-muscles on his sides before turning my focus to what's standing at attention between us.

"Sit on the bed," I demand, and he lifts a playful eyebrow at my tone but does what I say. I kneel down in front of him, my eyes zeroed in on how large his cock looks. I spread his knees apart, my hands sliding up his inner thighs until they wrap around him.

"You want this, baby?" His voice is husky, his eyes dark with passion.

I lick my lips and give him a slow, seductive smile. "Yeah."

He draws in a shaky breath while watching me kiss the tip, my hands massaging his shaft as I continue my slow torture. I start to lick him, my tongue concentrating fully on his tip. I take a look at him and gain more confidence when I see his head is thrown back, eyes closed, and his mouth parted in passion. I grow bolder, taking him deeper in my mouth, while I move up and down using suction on each downward glide. I never knew oral sex could be so much fun, so powerful, and I moan at how much I love giving it to him.

His hips start to rotate back and forth, his breathing harder and faster as he feels his tip reach the back of my throat. "Baby, this isn't how I want to come in you for the first time." He tugs on my hair and pulls my head back away from him. "Come here and climb on top of me." He scoots back until he's propped up against my pillows. I stand up, kneel on the bed, and crawl over to him. I get up on my knees and pull my dress up and over my head. His eyes drink me in from my black strapless bra down the rest of my very naked body.

"You're fucking gorgeous, baby," he growls while reaching for me and pulls me onto his lap, his dick pressing in between us. He starts kissing my neck, his hot breath giving me goose bumps as his hands trail up my back to the clasps of my bra. As soon as my breasts are relieved from their confines, he cups them in his large palms and begins massaging them. I moan as he uses the pads of his thumbs to rub circles over my nipples before deciding to give the left breast his attention. He takes my hardened nipple into his mouth and sucks while flicking it with his tongue, the wicked sensation making my core tighten. He soon moves on to my other breast, and I can't help but start grinding myself against him, his tongue driving me to the brink of insanity. So consumed am I with his wicked mouth that I don't even feel his hand sliding between us until his fingers rub between my folds.

"I love how wet you are for me," he whispers in my ear before nipping and sucking on my lobe.

I lace my fingers through his hair and bring him back to my mouth, his tongue thrusting between my parted lips. I love the way he kisses me, how his tongue dances perfectly with mine. I moan louder, becoming completely engulfed in his flames. His fingers begin their assault on my clit, teasing against it, making me crave for him to be inside me.

"I need you, Gavin," I whimper, my walls pulsating with the need to feel him inside me.

"What do you need, darlin'?" he asks, his voice husky with pleasure. He rubs his fingers in and out of me, the friction of their roughness making me quiver. "Tell me what you need, Aly."

"I need you inside me, now, baby."

He chuckles at my demand and removes his fingers. Without hesitation, I reach between us and grab him, guiding him to my entrance. I lift my pelvis up before I slowly slide down, both of us gasping at how amazing it feels. We stay still and just kiss each other so I can get used to having him inside me. But like usual, his kisses ignite the fire and I start moving against him.

"Baby, do I need to put a condom on?" He pants when he breaks our kiss. I shake my head, unable to concentrate on anything besides how good he feels inside me.

"I'm on birth control," I breathe out. "God, you feel so good," I murmur as I lift my torso up and steady myself by placing my hands against his abs. He grips the sides of my hips, his fingers digging into my flesh to help guide me. I start off by grinding against him, the friction against my clit making me purr. Needing more, I ride him harder, my hands grabbing my breasts and pinching my nipples.

"Fuck me, baby," he demands, his hips matching the rhythm of my own, causing the bedframe to slam repeatedly against the wall. He moves one hand off my hip and uses his thumb to rub against my clit, sending me into overdrive. The pressure of his thumb against me combined with my walls grasping around his thick cock skyrockets me over the edge.

"Ah yes, *yes!*" I scream out as the most powerful orgasm I've ever experienced rocks me to my core. My body is convulsing from the high when I feel him jerk up and yell out his own release. I collapse on top of him, unable to move off as I try to catch my breath. He wraps his arms around me and hugs me tightly to him.

"Damn, baby... if this is what sex is like

with you every time, then I'm going to be dying a very young man." His chest rumbles with laughter and I giggle, smiling at the beautiful sound and understanding exactly what he is feeling. The connection we have is raw, hungry, passionate… *meaningful*.

I listen to his heartbeat slowly come down to its normal rhythm, and I say a silent prayer of thanks for this man, hoping I get to listen to his heart like this every night from now on. Gavin McNeer better be mine to keep for the rest of my life, because he's completely ruined me for anyone else.

Thirteen

ALY

I CROSS ANOTHER item off my to-do list, sighing at what a hectic week it's been so far. Things at work have been so busy that I haven't had much time to reflect on how incredible the last couple days with Gavin have been. Multiple nights spent with him have convinced me that he's the only person I want to be with for the rest of my existence. I've never felt this connected with someone, mind, body, and soul.

When I sit down and really analyze that thought, I'm not scared by it. I'm one hundred percent confident what I'm feeling is genuine and not just lust. Every time we're together, our chemistry is off the charts, but beyond that, he makes me laugh, makes me happy, and is the most thoughtful, caring man I've ever met.

Tuesday was our one-week anniversary, and usually, that isn't something to celebrate, but Gavin said we needed to. I took a half day off work and we decided to go for a hike in Edwin Warner Park, since it was such a gorgeous day. We hiked for about two miles and stopped to have a picnic. Later that evening, he took me out to Pinewood Social, a trendy bowling alley, where we bowled and ate dinner. I love that he's just as silly as I am and we can have a good time no matter what we're doing.

Every night with him has been some sort of dream, but the best part of it all is it's just really easy being with him. I can be myself and not worry about whether or not I need to impress him. I always felt I needed to do something extra in order to keep my ex-boyfriend around. I would catch him eyeing other girls, and it always made me feel anxious, pressuring myself to make him satisfied. I didn't realize until after we broke up that he was never concerned about how I felt.

Gavin goes above and beyond to make me happy, and I never feel any pressure to have to be more for him. I just can't get over how quickly this is all happening. I only start to second-guess myself when talking to Valerie. She thinks I'm bat-shit crazy, especially after I told her at lunch yesterday that I think I'm in love with him.

"Are you high right now?" she practically screamed at me while we were eating. If our schedules permit, we try to meet up once a week during our breaks to eat lunch together and catch up.

"Jesus, Valerie, will you lower your voice?" I hissed while looking around to see our tablemates next to us giving us dirty looks. "And no, I'm not high."

"I swear to God, Alyson, if you've gotten into drugs because of that man, I will castrate him." She waved her fork at me, small pieces of food debris going all over the place.

Her ridiculous empty threat made me chuckle and I shook my head at her. "I'm clean as a whistle, sister. Want me to pee in this cup for you?" I joke, holding up my empty water cup for her.

She leaned forward and said in a soft voice, "How can you be in love with someone you just met a week ago? Do you know how crazy you sound?"

"Yes, I'm well aware of how crazy it sounds, but Val, I've never felt this way for someone before."

"Aly, you've only had two boyfriends in your whole life and they were in high school and college. There's nothing to compare!" Her annoyed expression angered me, because she had no room to talk with her non-existent love life.

"You know what, Val? Until you've felt what I'm feeling, your opinion doesn't matter," I told her, wishing she would just be supportive instead of being so judgmental.

"Felt what? Love?" she asked in mock-confusion.

I put my fork down and tried to think of the proper words to describe my feelings for Gavin. "Not just any kind of love—a soul wrenching, wrapping-its-claws-around-your-heart kind of love the instant your eyes catch each other's." I smiled at the thought of him, his handsome face and heart-melting smile springing into my mind. I finally realized I wasn't paying attention and shifted my gaze back to her. The look of I-don't-understand-a-word-you-just-said was written all over her face.

I threw my hands up in the air, annoyed she couldn't understand what I was describing. "You know, that feeling that you can't live without someone? When you see them, your heart starts to pound like crazy?" She starts to shake her head and I scrambled to think of a better description.

"You know... like a shazam!" I said loudly, throwing my hands into her face and scaring her to the point she jumped.

Unfortunately, my shazam analogy didn't convince her and she voiced her concerns to my mother, who didn't even know Gavin existed in my world. Both of my parents are not big country music fans, so they had no idea he's actually a celebrity. They have demanded I bring him over for family dinner on Sunday. I wasn't planning on introducing him to them so soon, but now that they know about him, better to get the introductions out of the way. I know my mother will quickly fall for his charm and see how wonderful he is, but my father's a different story. Whatever his reaction may be to Gavin, I couldn't care less. No one is going to convince me otherwise that I shouldn't be with him.

"How we doing over there, sunshine?"

Shane's question interrupts my thoughts, and I look up from my computer to smile at him.

"We're doing excellent," I say confidently while looking him in the eye.

"I swear you are glowing so brightly that you're about to burn my eyes out. Looks like my little Aly has done the nasty with Mr. McNeer." I shake my head at him and try to keep a straight face but can't control the blush that stains my cheeks. He throws his head back and laughs hysterically at my reaction. "Thank you to your cheeks for answering my question."

I throw my notebook at him, causing him to laugh even more. Seeing that nothing is going to stop the hyena like sounds, I choose to ignore him instead.

He takes a couple deep breaths and

composes himself before asking, "Are we all set for the game tonight?"

"We sure are," I confirm. "Food and beverages have been ordered for the suite and all personalized jerseys are in."

Shane decided to use some of his marketing budget to get his staff and the artists who are attending tonight's game personalized jerseys. I added some to the order for Gavin, Sosie, and Willow, paying for theirs out of my own pocket. I'm excited for tonight, especially to see how Willow and Brodie get along. I sent Brodie a text this morning, letting him know we'll be at the game and inviting him out to meet us for drinks afterward. Fortunately, the team isn't flying back to Detroit tonight, so he agreed to meet us at the rooftop bar across from the arena after the game.

"Wonderful, thank you. Let's put the jerseys in gift bags and we'll hand them out to everyone when they arrive in the suite," Shane tells me before walking away from my desk.

Excitement is buzzing throughout the office for tonight. It's the first round of the Stanley Cup Playoffs and the Predators are tied with Detroit in the series. It's crucial that the Preds win tonight and then try to win the next game in Detroit if they want to advance to the next round in the playoffs.

I grab a stack of our branded gift bags and tissue paper we keep on hand from the supply closet and start wrapping the jerseys in the paper before putting them into the bags and writing that person's name on the outside. I'm halfway through when I hear the sound of someone's high-heeled shoes coming toward me. I look up to see Kathleen Davidson standing in front of me.

"Hello, Aly," she greets me with a nod. She's an attractive woman in her late forties, who takes care of herself by working out. Her youthful appearance is courtesy of Botox and fillers, and her straight, red hair is made up of the best extensions money can buy. I've always admired her style of clothes, and today is no exception with her lacy, emerald-green tunic, skin-tight black leather pants, and black, pointy heels I recognize as Louboutins with their red bottoms.

"Hello, Mrs. Davidson, how are you?" I ask, my smile overly bright to cover up how shocked I am that she knows my name.

"Oh please, call me Kathleen." She laughs, waving her hand in the air.

"Okay... Kathleen." I look behind me at Shane's open door to see he isn't back in his office. "Shane is around here somewhere. Do you want me to tell him to go see you in your office when he returns?"

"Actually, you're the one I wanted to see. Do you have a moment to chat?"

My eyes widen in surprise at her request. Kathleen Davidson doesn't spend alone time with A&R assistants. Anything she needs gets streamlined down through the A&R directors and managers. A knot in my stomach forms, my intuition screaming at me that she wants to discuss my new relationship with Gavin.

Please, God, don't have her tell me to break up with him.

"Sure," I say and follow her back to her office, which is upstairs on the second floor. She stops at her door and gestures with her arm for me to go inside. I walk past her, and she shuts the door behind us.

"Please, have a seat and make yourself comfortable."

I obey and sit down while she walks

around her desk to sit in her own seat. I've never been to her office before, and I glance around, admiring her decor. Her large office is decorated in a charcoal, gold, and white color palette. My eyes follow around the platinum albums of past and present artists of Big Little Music that decorate the walls. Her accomplishments are impressive in an industry that is predominantly ran by men.

"You're office is gorgeous," I tell her while I continue looking around in awe.

"Thank you! My favorite part is seeing all the beautiful, blingy records on the walls," she says laughing. I smile while studying her, hoping she cuts to the chase soon, so I don't have to sit and make small talk with her.

"Well, Aly, I know you're busy, so I'll make this brief. I've heard you're dating Gavin McNeer. Is that true?" Her tone of voice turns business-like, her eyes studying me for my reaction.

"Yes, it's true. Is there a problem?" I ask, matching her tone in what I hope shows that I'm not intimidated by her.

"No, of course not. I just wanted confirmation to come from you. Pictures on the Internet can be so deceiving."

I nod in agreement, silently wondering where this conversation is going.

"I also wanted to check in and see how you're doing under all the scrutiny of dating a celebrity. A couple members of the paparazzi were waiting for you outside the office this morning when I arrived." She holds up her hand at my horrified expression. "Now, don't worry; I told them this was private property and would call the police on them if they show up here again."

"Thank you for doing that, Mrs. Davidson... I mean, Kathleen," I say with sincerity. I hate the fact that these kinds of people are showing up at my work. I've enjoyed not having social media anymore, and I have refrained from googling myself and Gavin. "I'm sorry for the disturbance."

"It's not your fault; it comes with the territory of dating someone famous. I just wanted to make sure you were handling it okay."

"To be quite honest, I don't enjoy the attention, but it's just something I will have to get used to."

"Right," she agrees and smiles at me with sympathy. "And how is Gavin handling this newfound fame? Being a well-known songwriter doesn't have the attention that a performer in front of big crowds and cameras does."

"He doesn't enjoy the loss of privacy, but otherwise, he's great."

"Glad to hear this," she says, folding her hands together and leaning back in her chair. "Are the people at Charisma still treating him well?"

"As far as I know, yes, but we don't usually talk business." I tilt my head to the side and look at her in confusion. "With all due respect, Kathleen, why are you asking?"

"I personally have had to deal with Atticus Langston before and know firsthand what a treacherous human being he can be. I just didn't want to hear that Gavin is being ostracized there, since he's not dating Atticus's daughter anymore." She glances down at her manicure before continuing. "We would never do anything like that here, and I think it's important for Gavin to know he has options if he ever starts to feel that way."

I narrow my eyes at her, not liking the direction this conversation is going. "What do you mean by options?"

She smiles, sits up, and leans in closer. "Imagine how wonderful life would be if Gavin signed with us? We would promote you to be his A&R manager, so you can be there every step of the way with him on his future albums. Because he would be such an important client, we could arrange it so that you would only have one other client besides him. You would be invested in him both personally and professionally."

Bile starts to rise up my throat, and I have to force myself to swallow it down. "I prefer not to mix business with pleasure," I tell her coldly as I stand up, signaling I'm ready to end this conversation and leave.

"This would be the next stepping stone for your career, Aly." She smiles at me, but I don't return one back. "No harm in thinking about it. After all, you want what's best for the both of you, right?" she questions with a raised eyebrow, a sly smile playing on her lips.

Shane said Kathleen can be a shark when she needs to be. I just never would have guessed I would be the one she would prey on. She stands up and walks around her desk to open the door for me.

"Thank you for all of your hard work for us, Aly. Shane raves about you and we're lucky to have someone so dedicated to her job. You have a very bright future with us ahead of you." I nod and give her a stiff smile as I walk past her to leave.

"Oh, and Aly?" I turn around to look at her when she calls out my name. "Please make sure to introduce me to Gavin tonight when we're all at the game. See you later!" She smiles one more time and then closes her door.

I storm back to my office, my emotions turbulent on what just occurred. With it almost being five o'clock and Shane still not back in his office, I decide I deserve to leave early to get ready for tonight. I leave him a note and grab my belongings, needing to get out of this place to calm down and think about how to handle this.

♡ ♡ ♡ ♡ ♡ ♡

GAVIN INVITED ME to spend the night at his house after the game, so I head home. There are a few things I need to take care of around my place; plus, I need to pack my bag and change for tonight. Sosie is supposed to be meeting us at Gavin's, so the three of us can ride to the game together—something I'm not exactly looking forward to. I tried to convince Willow to meet us as well, hoping she could be a little bit of a buffer, but she couldn't get off work early. She'll meet us outside of the arena and we'll all walk in together, since I have everyone's ticket.

After I accomplish everything I need to do at home and have packed my bag, I change into jeans and a cute tunic with booties, since it's cold in the arena, and freshen up my makeup. I give Apollo some extra attention and love, since I won't be home tonight, feed him, and leave for Gavin's.

While I'm excited to finally see his place, I'm also still bothered by my conversation with Kathleen. There's no way in hell I'm going to try to convince Gavin to sign with Big Little Music when his contract with Charisma is up. I don't want Gavin to have any doubts about me and my motives for being with him. Trying to get him to my record label would throw up red flags. I think it's best not to tell him what happened, so that way there's no awkwardness between him and Kathleen whenever they run in to each other, which happens quite frequently at industry events.

I silence the warning bells going off in my head that I should be one hundred percent honest with Gavin on this. If our relationship wasn't so new, I would call him up and tell him right now. But it isn't, and until I know he trusts me completely, I will stay silent on this matter. As for Kathleen, I'll just ignore her as long as possible before she brings the subject up again.

Satisfied with my plan, I focus on my drive to his apartment, which takes me less than ten minutes to get to. I get lucky and find street parking across from his building. I grab my belongings out of my trunk and cross the street. Gavin lives in one of the new, trendy high-rise apartment complexes that just got built two years ago. I hit the intercom button outside the front door and wait for someone to answer.

"Can I help you?" I look through the glass windows of the door to see the doorman looking at me, a phone pressed to his ear so he can hear me talk through the intercom.

"Hi, I'm here to see Gavin McNeer."

"Name?"

"Alyson Dawson." He looks at something behind his desk and nods.

"Come on in. Please have your driver's license ready for me to look at."

A loud buzzing noise sounds and I pull the door open to enter. I walk over to his station and hand him my driver's license. He types my information into his computer and hands it back to me.

"Mr. McNeer has put you on his approved guest list. Please type in your own personal four-digit code for you to use on the outside keypad to get in. After you have your code, please hit the pound sign." He produces a keypad that is connected to his computer, and I type in four digits I know I will remember. I hit the pound sign and tell him I'm done. "Now please enter your cell phone number." Once I'm done, he takes the keypad back and I hear his mouse clicking a couple more times until he's finished. "You're all set, Ms. Dawson. Elevators are around the corner to my right, and Mr. McNeer is on the fourteenth floor, apartment 1405."

I thank him for his help and walk to the elevators. The decor in the lobby is very cold and modern, making me wonder why Gavin chose this building, since that doesn't seem to fit his personality. Yet again, I could be completely wrong, since this is my first time seeing his place. I push the up button and the doors to my right open immediately. The ride to up is quick and quiet. The elevators slows to a stop and the doors open to reveal one handsome-looking Texan leaning against the frame, waiting for me.

"There's my girl," he says in his yummy, husky voice. He grabs my wrists and pulls me out of the elevator straight into his arms. His lips come down on mine, his tongue immediately demanding entrance through my parted lips.

I sigh in happiness as I kiss him back with equal vigor. Lord, this man knows how to kiss, and after a few moments, all brain and body activity is focused on him. I drop my bags to the ground and wrap my arms around his neck to pull him in deeper. I feel his hands slide into the back pockets of my jeans, cupping my ass, and rubbing me against his erection. I moan at how good the friction feels, my body aching for him to be inside me.

I wonder if we have time for a quickie.

"Sosie got here early, and I could fucking kill her for it. It was my plan to ravish you before we left," he tells me in between kisses, as if he's reading my damn mind. "There might be a janitor closet somewhere on this floor." He gives me an evil smile with a wink before continuing his assault on my lips.

"Tonight," I say breathlessly, releasing my hold on him so I can start getting control over myself.

"You bet that fine ass of yours *tonight*," he growls, giving me one last hard peck on the lips before pulling his hands out of my pockets. He picks up my duffle bag from the floor and then eyes the three gift bags. "What are those?" he asks, pointing to them.

"Surprises," I say vaguely, giving him a mysterious smile. I pick up the three bags off the floor and shake my head at him when he tries to carry them for me.

"Darlin', you're the only present I'll ever

want." He grabs my free hand and leads me down a hallway to his apartment.

"Well, that's no fun because you already have me." I squeeze his hand in mine and we come to a stop in front of his door. He brings our joined hands up to his lips and kisses my knuckles.

"I hope so," he whispers and softly kisses me on my mouth. When he pulls back, I see a look in his eyes I've never seen before. It's filled with tenderness and, dare I hope… love?

Please, God, let him be falling just as hard and fast as I am.

He gives me a reassuring smile and opens the door to his apartment. He pulls me into his place and lets go of my hand to close the door behind us, giving me the opportunity to look around. Light-gray paint coats the walls, and the first thing that catches my eye is the floor-to-ceiling windows showcasing a gorgeous view of the city. High ceilings create the illusion of a bigger place than what the square footage actually is.

I walk farther in and look to my right at the kitchen with dark cabinets, white quartz countertops, and stainless-steel appliances.

Two industrial-looking chandeliers hang over the island. In front of me is the living room with rustic wood beams on the ceiling, a small, black leather sectional couch that Sosie is sitting on, working on her computer, and a very large television hanging inside a built-in entertainment unit on the opposite wall.

"Say hello, Sosie," Gavin says, his tone sounding like a father reprimanding their child.

"Hello, Sosie," she mimics, not even bothering to look up.

"Don't be a bitch," he growls in anger, causing her head to snap up in surprise, and that's when she notices me.

"Sorry, I didn't know she came in with you." She pushes her red glasses up her nose and looks at me. "Hello, Alyson." I want to roll my eyes but instead bite my lip to keep from reacting. She might act like she's hard as nails, but I believe Gavin is right about her and I have no doubt her aversion to me is all an act to protect her heart from possibly getting hurt by anyone she might let in.

"Pain in my fucking ass," he grumbles underneath his breath, and I want to tell him it's okay, but I keep my mouth closed. "Let me show you my bedroom." He grabs my bag, and I follow him across the apartment.

His bedroom isn't very big, but it does have the same amazing view of the city as the living room. The only furniture in the small space is his king-sized bed in a large, mahogany bedframe, two matching nightstands with lamps, and a ceiling fan overhead.

"Over there is the bathroom." He nods toward a closed door. "And in here is the master closet."

I follow him down the slight hallway to the closet and step inside. It's almost as big as his kitchen and is customized with shelves, drawers, and cubbies. I immediately have closet envy and wish mine was as big and as organized as this one. "I, um... cleared out a drawer for you." He rubs the back of his neck and casts his eyes downward, appearing unsure for the very first time since I've known him.

I walk over to him and wrap my arms around his torso, squeezing him in appreciation. "Thank you," I whisper as I lean up on my tippy toes to kiss him. "I look forward to putting things in it." I touch my smiling lips to his in what was only going to be a soft kiss, but when his fingers thread through my hair and hold me in place, the kiss goes from soft and tender to hard and hungry in less than five seconds. It's always like this with him—this overwhelming feeling to be completely devoured by him. I love it and am scared by it, all at the same time.

I love this feeling, because it makes me feel wanted, like he can't get enough of me and always wants more.

I'm scared by it, because what if this doesn't work out and I never have this feeling for someone ever again? I can't even imagine finding someone else who makes me feel the way Gavin does.

Soon, his touch and scent make me forget my inhibitions and all I want is him inside me. He pins me against the drawers and hoists me up. My legs instinctively wrap around his waist, and I moan at the familiar pressure that starts to build every time I feel him rub against me.

"So fucking sweet," he groans before claiming my mouth again with his.

I sigh in delicious contentment, enjoying this moment and only acknowledging what really matters to me—him and us.

"Your animal noises are starting to do permanent damage to my brain! Stop sucking face and let's get out of here!" Sosie yells at us from the kitchen, snapping us back into reality.

We pull away from each other, but our foreheads touch as we attempt to catch our breaths.

"I think we should revoke her invitation to the game," he says, and I laugh at his frustration with his cousin as he puts me back down on my feet.

"We can't leave just yet." I grab my Predators jersey out of my duffle bag and put it on over my shirt. "You need to open your present before we go." I smile up at him as we walk back out into the living room together and see Sosie standing by the door, her bag on her shoulder, ready to go. I grab the three gift bags and hand one to Gavin and one to Sosie.

"What's this for?" Sosie asks, holding the handle of the bag with the tips of her fingers as if it's coated with an infectious disease.

"It something fun for you to wear tonight,"

I tell her before turning all my attention to Gavin while he opens up the bag and takes out his jersey.

"Darlin', you didn't have to do this." He flips the jersey over to see his last name personalized on the back. "Baby, this is amazing." He puts the jersey on, and I'm happy to see it fits like a glove. He crushes me into a bear hug and kisses me hard on the lips. "I fucking love it. Thank you, baby." I'm rewarded with one more kiss before he lets me go, feeling completely breathless and once again, turned on.

"Why would you buy this for me?" Sosie asks, and I turn to find a look of confusion written across her face as she holds up her jersey.

"Because we need to show support for the home team," I reply, and she looks at me doubtfully. "And, it's always fun to receive presents." I shrug. I don't understand her or why she's acting so unappreciative, but I refuse to let her put me in a bad mood. I do make a mental note never to buy her another present again.

"I know my mother taught you better

manners than that," Gavin snaps in anger at Sosie and her attitude. "These jersey and the tickets we got tonight are courtesy of Aly and her company. If you can't be even a little appreciative, then don't fucking come with us."

I squeeze his hand in a silent signal letting him know I'm fine. I appreciate him coming to my defense, but he doesn't need to be so harsh with her. I give Sosie an apologetic smile, but she just stands there and continues staring at me. "You don't have to wear it," I say, cutting through the uncomfortable silence.

"I'll wear it. Thank you for thinking of me," she says after a moment, her voice softer than I've ever heard it.

I nod in acknowledgement and smile brightly between the two of them, hoping to lighten the mood. "Come on, let's go have some fun tonight!"

I don't even bother checking to see if she puts on the jersey. I grab my purse and Willow's bag off the counter, lace my fingers with Gavin's, and head toward the door. As long as I get to come home with Gavin tonight, nothing else matters.

Fourteen

GAVIN

$\mathcal{T}$HE NOISE LEVEL inside the arena is at a loud enough decibel that it rings through your veins, making your heart pound in your chest from the excitement of the game. There's nothing like playoff hockey, and tonight the arena is colored in yellow with fans rocking their jerseys in support of the home team.

The game is tied 2-2, with the first period just about to end.

"I'm gonna get some food. You want anything?" I ask Aly, who's been chatting with Willow throughout the game.

"Not right now." She smiles as the horn

sounds.

"I'll be back." I kiss her swiftly on the lips and then walk myself over to the buffet. I help myself to a plate of food, grab a beer, and stand at the nearest high-top table to eat and people-watch.

The suite is packed with employees and artists from Big Little Music, all hanging out, laughing, eating, and having a good time. Aly introduced me to everyone when we arrived. Most of the Big Little Music employees I've never met, but some of their artists who are here I already knew, like Scotty Wilkins. The only person Aly didn't seem too keen on me meeting was their owner, Kathleen Davidson.

I noticed Aly lost the warm look in her eyes she normally carries when she made that introduction. Since we've met, she's raved about how much she loves her job, especially her boss, Shane, so her reaction to Kathleen surprised me. I shake away the thought but make a mental note to ask her about it later when we're alone.

I look over at her and can't stop the smile that spreads across my face when I see her laughing at something Willow says. After meeting Willow Mayson and listening to those two chat during the game, I can see why she and Aly are best friends. Both women radiate warmth and happiness and shine it down on anyone who is lucky enough to be in their presence. They are gorgeous, but so down to earth that they are unaware of their beauty. Smart, yet love to be silly. Generous, but won't put up with anyone's shit if they are trying to take advantage of them.

It's surprising to me that someone like Willow is single, but then again, so was Aly when I met her. I just hope Aly's matchmaking skills tonight don't backfire on her. She told me and Sosie her plans to play matchmaker between Willow and her hockey player friend, Brodie. Thank fuck this guy is just a friend and not someone she dated. I wouldn't be able to be in the same room as him if I knew his hands were ever on my girl.

The sounds of a band starting to play pull me out of my thoughts. I finish eating, throw away my plate, and return to my seat next to Aly to watch the entertainment for the first intermission.

"No shit," I say to myself but loud enough

for Aly to turn to me and ask what's wrong. "I know those guys," I tell her, pointing to the band. "Harry and the Seahawks used to be legends as the Friday night entertainment at this bar on Demonbreun Street. Their energy is amazing, probably one of the best cover bands around." I listen to them rock an Aerosmith song and can't stop from bobbing my head to their beat.

"Do they still play there? We should all go sometime if they do," Aly suggests, looking between me and Willow, who nods in agreement.

"I don't know. Harry and I kind of lost touch. I still have his number though, so let me send him a text saying hello." I pull out my phone from my pocket to send him a text, letting him know I'm here and they're killing it. Once the text is sent, I put my phone away and grab Aly's hand, linking our fingers together.

We continue watching Harry and his band for the remainder of his set and cheer loudly for them when they finish. Movement out of the corner of my right eye catches my attention, and I look over to see Sosie coming back to her seat next to me with a beer in hand and Scotty Wilkins following behind her. His gaze is downward while he concentrates on Sosie walking in front of him.

Is that asshole staring at my cousin's ass?

I narrow my eyes at Scotty, and as if he can feel the burning of my gaze, he looks up at me right before he sits down next to her. I point two of my fingers to my eyes and flip them around to him, letting him know I'm watching him. He gives me a smirk, and that only pisses me off even more. Not wanting to cause a scene and embarrass Aly, I let go of her hand to retrieve my phone and send him a text.

Me: Don't even think about it, motherfucker.

Scotty: Might be more like cousinfucker. *laughing emoji

My head snaps up, daggers shooting out of my eyes at him, as my self-control to not punch his face in is about to snap. The buzzing of my phone with an incoming text just might have saved his life.

Scotty: Cool your tits, McNeer. I was only kidding. Sosie and I are just friends. She's like a little sister to me.

I snort at his comment. He must think I'm a dumbass, because there's no way in hell he views Sosie as his little sister. Brothers don't ogle their sister's ass like he just did hers.

I look at Sosie to see how she's doing, and to my surprise, a smile is on her face. *Shit*, Sosie might actually be having fun tonight. I watch her take a sip of her beer and wonder how many of those she's had and if that's why she's in a good mood. Scotty points out something to her on the ice and she laughs. The sound is real and genuine, something I haven't heard out of her for a very long time. I decide to let Scotty's comment go… for now. But know that he and I are going to have a little chat at our jam session next week.

The sound of the second period horn blares and my attention is brought back to the game as the puck drops. Both teams start the period out sluggish, but when the Red Wings score their third goal, it seems to light a fire beneath the Predators. They come on strong for the next ten minutes, smoking past the defense and taking shot after shot at the Red Wings goaltender, who plays phenomenally. He finally lets one slip past his pads and it's none other than Brodie Larsen, who scores the goal to tie the game back up. Aly jumps out of her seat in excitement, cheering loudly for Brodie.

"Babe, did you see that? How cool is it that Brodie just tied it up?"

I laugh at her infectious excitement, my gaze dropping down to that beautiful smile of hers. A smile that makes me feel happy and alive every time I see it. A lump of emotions lodges in my throat as I look at her, and an overwhelming need to tell her how important she is to me starts to form. The feel of my cell vibrating in my pocket distracts me from my thoughts, and I pull it out to see I have a text from Harry.

Harry: Hey, man, great to hear from you. Thanks for the kind words. Let's get together and jam soon.

I'm about to text him back, asking him to send me his schedule, when an idea pops in my head, making my eyes widen. It might embarrass the hell out of Aly, but in the end, if I can pull this off, it would be one of the best ways to publicly tell her how much she means to me. A mischievous smile forms on my lips and I text Harry back.

Me: How do you feel about jamming together in about fifteen minutes? Mind if I crash your second intermission set?

A small part of me feels like a selfish prick for asking, considering this is his gig, but his quick response back to me diminishes any guilt I had for asking.

Harry: Fuck yeah! Let's do it. Meet me outside of Section 111 as soon as the second period ends, and I'll bring you on stage with us.

I squeeze my fist in excitement, thankful that Harry is going to help me out. I look up at the scoreboard to see we have ten more minutes left in the period which in sports, can mean another thirty minutes with all the stops in between plays. Time seems to move more slowly, and I start to get antsy, unable to control my right leg from bouncing every few seconds with nervous energy.

"Gavin, your bouncing is driving me insane. What's wrong with you? Do we need to take you to a doctor or something? You get like this every time you're about to perform." Damn Sosie for being so fucking loud, because now Aly is looking at me and my leg in concern.

"It's okay, baby." I give her a reassuring smile. "This game is just so exciting that I can't sit still," I lie through my teeth and start cheering "Let's Go, Predators!" with the crowd, hoping I'm giving a convincing performance. Once she sees I'm okay, she turns her attention back to the game.

"Sos." I lean closer to her so she can hear me over the loud sounds of the game. "When the band starts to play during the second intermission, I need you to record Aly's reaction."

"And why would I want to do that?" She leans back to look at me and narrows her eyes when she notices the wicked gleam in mine. "What are you planning, Gavin?"

"You'll see." I smirk, loving how the suspense of her not knowing what I'm up to is killing her.

Finally, the scoreboard reads five minutes left in the second period and I decide this is my time to make my move. I turn to Aly, grab her chin so she faces me, and kiss her before explaining. "Some friends of mine saw I was here when they announced it on the jumbotron and texted me to come say hello to them downstairs. I'm going to run there now before the crowd starts up during intermission. Be right back."

"Sure." She smiles at me and nods in acknowledgement before turning her attention back to the game when the crowd starts to cheer.

I leave the suite and text Harry that I'm on my way down. I should've taken into account the amount of time I'd spend with fans wanting pictures or me to sign shit, but this whole being famous business is still new to me. By the time I make it down to Section 111, Harry and his band are waiting for me.

"Good to see you, man," I say after shaking all their hands and embracing Harry in a hug. "Thanks for letting me crash your gig."

"Are you kidding? We're fucking honored to have you on stage with us. Do you want to stay for the whole set or just one song?" he asks.

"Just one song, and here's what I had in mind." I tell him the song I want to perform, and his eyes light up with excitement.

"Nice! That song is a classic and we've performed it in the past. This crowd is going to go nuts," he says, and his bandmates all nod in agreement. The sound of the horn interrupts us, indicating it's now the end of the second period. "We'll perform first and then bring you on as a surprise guest. Cool?"

"Let's do it!" I say eagerly, slapping Harry's back in excitement for what's about to come. "Knock em' dead, boys!"

I follow the band through the small tunnel and stand back to the side, so I'm not seen. I peek my head around the wall to see how far away the suite is from the stage. The suite is closer to the middle of the ice on my right side but not too far that I wouldn't be able to see if Aly is watching. Fortunately, she's still sitting in her seat and is talking to Shane and Willow. I resume my position behind the wall and watch the band take the stage. Their keyboardist starts playing the opening chords to "Don't Stop Believin'" by Journey, and the crowd erupts in cheers of appreciation. They use the song to pump the crowd up and it works. As I gaze out around the packed arena, I notice people singing and some standing to dance. The band finishes the song and I slowly start making my way to the stage.

"Nashville, are you ready for one more song before the Preds bury the Red Wings in the third period?" Harry asks the crowd, who cheers loudly. "We have a special guest joining us for this last song. Give a loud welcome to Mr. Gavin McNeer!"

I walk forward and wave at the crowd, ecstatic to see they're clapping for me. I nod at the guitarist to start the opening guitar chord of "Somebody Like You" by Keith Urban. I grip the microphone, since I'm not the one playing the guitar, and look over at the suite. I chuckle when I see Aly, Willow, and Shane standing up, with Shane and Willow jumping up and down, shaking Aly, who is covering her mouth with her hands in shock.

"This is for my girl, Aly," I yell into the microphone and point to her. I see Sosie recording Aly with her phone, and I'm grateful she listened. Everyone in the suite has now crowded around Aly to watch my performance, clapping and cheering me on as I start the first verse.

I soon lose myself in the lyrics, and quickly realize how perfect this song really is for the story of us. It was a huge hit back in its day, and I've sung it before, but it wasn't until tonight that I can appreciate the beauty of its words. It's about finding that special person who makes you better than what you were. That you feel happier being around them and that their confidence in you makes you believe in yourself. When you find that person who makes you feel that way, you want to love them and be loved in return. Standing here, singing this song for her, the lyrics mean everything to me, because she's exactly that kind of person. She's the somebody I want to love, and I want to love her until I breathe my last breath. I was destined to sing this song to her, to be the man who loves her unconditionally and make her dreams come true.

The crowd is on their feet as we come to the guitar solo. Harry and his band perform the song seamlessly. After the solo, I signal the band to slow it down and get the crowd to sing along with me, and then sing the chorus by itself. The moment is pure magic, and when I look over at Aly, I see her swipe at her cheeks as if she's crying.

"*I want to love you, baby,*" I sing into the mic, and the crowd goes wild. We end the song with a bang, and I thank the crowd then yell, "Let's go, Preds!" before high-fiving the band and hugging Harry. I'm ecstatic at how the performance went, and I seriously couldn't have pulled it off without Harry and his band. As we exit the stage, I promise him we'll catch up soon with lunch before saying goodbye.

I exit the tunnel and start to walk briskly back to the suite. I should have thought about an exit strategy after that epic performance. I'm stopped numerous times by fans wanting an autograph, photo, or just to talk. I hear the sound of the horn for the third period and realize I haven't moved for the last five minutes. Another five minutes go by before security comes to my rescue, seeing how large the crowd was getting around me. I apologize to the fans who I didn't get to take a photo with and am escorted back to the suite. As soon as the door opens, everyone starts applauding and rushing toward me. Scotty Wilkins is the first person who approaches, embracing me and pounding me on my back.

"Can you fucking tone it down, dude? You're making it hard for us other men."

I laugh at him, since he has no trouble

getting the ladies with his good looks and charm. Which is exactly why I want him to stay far away from my cousin.

"All seriousness, Gav. She's a good girl. Don't fuck it up," he warns me with a serious look in his eye.

"I have no intention of letting her go," I respond with my own seriousness.

He nods in acknowledgement. "I'll see you around. I've got some other people to say hi to. I'll see you at Ripley's." He says goodbye and leaves the suite.

The rest of the people standing around congratulate me on an amazing performance, and I plaster a smile on my face and try to make my way to Aly, whose head I can barely see in back of the crowd. Finally, the sea of people parts and time seems to stop as she walks toward me with tears spilling from her eyes and down her cheeks. I open my arms and she embraces me, burying her face into my chest.

"What did you think, baby?" I ask, wrapping my fingers around her jaw and lifting her chin up with my fingers so I can stare into her eyes. At first, I'm worried she's embarrassed that I dedicated the song publicly to her and hold my breath.

"That was the most incredible thing anyone has ever done for me," she tells me, and my breath catches when I see happiness glowing back at me from her beautiful eyes.

"Thank fuck." I grin then groan when she grabs my face and pulls me forward to kiss me with raw, unashamed passion. We get lost in each other and it isn't until we hear someone tell us to get a room that we break away, breathing heavy.

I hold her face between my hands and look into her eyes, not giving a fuck who is watching us. "I meant every fucking word, Aly. Every. Single. One," I growl, referring to the words of the song, before giving her one more swift kiss. She's smiling as she nods at me, a silent promise filling her eyes that's telling me that tonight is just another memorable night in our future together.

♡♡♡♡♡♡

I LOOK AT my watch, feeling aggravated when I see it's only been five minutes since the last time I checked it. I'm ready to get the fuck out of here, but Aly refuses to leave her friend. I look across the table at Willow, who looks just as bored as I am. I can see she doesn't want to be here any longer and is completely unimpressed with Brodie Larsen, the guy Aly is trying to hook her up with. A man who's currently standing at the bar, talking to another woman, and has been for the last ten minutes.

We've been at Ripley's for an hour already, and the loud music and party atmosphere is starting to grate on my nerves. This was my scene when I first moved to Nashville—late nights at the bar, drinking, loud music, and trying to pick up women. The shit got old fast, and when I saw it was starting to affect my career, I went cold turkey, preferring to stay at home and work on my craft. Right now, I'd rather be buried deep inside my girl instead of being here.

"Babe, when are we leaving?" I ask Aly for the third time. Her eyes plead with me to stop asking and she bites her lip, making me growl out in frustration, because *I* want to be biting that lip.

"Yeah, I'm ready to go home too," Willow says, confirming another reason why I like her.

She's not into the party scene either. Willow tried to go straight home after the game, and Aly had to beg and plead with her to stay and have one drink with us. Willow pushes her chair back and stands up, causing Aly's eyes to widen in panic.

"Where are you going?" Aly tugs on her arm, attempting to urge her to sit back down, but Willow stands firm and pulls her arm out of Aly's grip.

"I'm going home. I'm tired and there's no reason for me to be here, not to mention your guy is ready to go."

"Please stay," Aly hisses and looks at me with weariness before speaking to Willow. "I really think you and Brodie might hit it off."

"Please tell me you're not trying to set me up with the douchebag over there who has barely said one word to us since he's gotten here." She glances at Brodie before she looks at Aly with an incredulous look.

"Maybe," Aly says, sounding unsure.

Willow snorts in disgust. "Seriously, Al? You thought I would be attracted to a guy like that?" She dismisses him with a wave of her hand and shakes her head. "I don't know if I should be really disappointed in you for thinking I'm that desperate or just pissed."

"Of course I know you're not desperate. Honestly, he usually doesn't act this way."

"How well do you really know him, Al? Because this is the first time I've ever heard you talk about him," Willow says, sitting down on the edge of her seat with a brow raised.

My girl starts to get flustered under Willow's scrutiny, and as entertaining as this shit is, my mind starts to focus on the noticeable absence of Sosie. I noticed at the game she had a lot to drink, so when we got to Ripley's, I told her to move to water so she wouldn't end up sick. A while ago, I saw her wander up to the bar, but I haven't seen her since. I scan the bar to where she last was but don't see her.

"Has anyone seen Sosie?" I ask the girls, who stop arguing to look at me. They both start looking around, and when they don't see her, they look at each other.

"I don't see her," Willow says, sounding worried.

"Willow, you go look in the ladies' room. Gavin, you search the area up here, and I'll go downstairs to look for her," Aly instructs us as we get up from our seats. While I don't like the idea of being separated from Aly, she's right in that we'll have a better chance of finding her if the three of us look in separate places. We all nod in agreement and split up to look for Sosie.

I take my phone out and send Sosie a message, telling her it's time to go home and meet us by the front door. I scour the second floor with no sign of her. I find Willow coming out of the restroom, and she shakes her head at me. We go downstairs and are able to find Aly leaning against the wall, watching the dance floor. I follow her line of vision to see Sosie embraced tightly in the arms of some guy, slow dancing.

"What the fuck?" I growl as I start to take a step toward them, when Aly grabs my arm to stop me.

"Look at her face, Gavin. She's having fun. Let her dance with a stranger for once and live a little."

"Fuck no, that guy could be a serial killer for all we know."

Aly laughs, wraps her arms around my waist, and squeezes. "We aren't going to let her go home with him. Let them finish out the song and then we will grab her to go. She's fine."

"There you guys are." We turn around to see Brodie standing next to us. "I've been looking for you and thought you ghosted me for a second."

"I'm surprised you even noticed we were gone," Willow says sarcastically, rolling her eyes.

"Obviously, I did or I wouldn't be standing here," Brodie points out.

"Whatever, don't do us any favors." Willow turns her back on him, and his eyes seem to focus on her like he's seeing her for the first time. Maybe I judged him too quickly back there. I know what it's like to be in the limelight. Maybe he was just trying to get a drink and got bombarded by people seeking his attention.

"Oh shit," I hear and turn to see Sosie practically falling out of the stranger's arms she was dancing with. I don't hesitate and push my way through the crowd to get her.

"Sosie, are you okay?" I ask as I reach out for her, and she falls into me. Murder blazes out of my eyes, because I'm going to kill someone.

"What the fuck did you do to my cousin?" I bellow in the guy's face. He holds up his hands and takes a step back, fear briefly flashing through his eyes.

"I didn't give her shit, man. She was like this when we started talking. Then she grabbed me and brought me out here to dance, so I thought I was helping her by holding her up."

"Get the fuck out of here," I tell him in a menacing voice, and he turns around and leaves right away. I throw one of Sosie's arms around my shoulders and grab her by the waist, making sure to walk slowly off the dance floor as she hisses that she's going to be sick.

"Oh my gosh! Sosie!" Aly runs up to us and gets on her other side to help hold her up. I look between Brodie and Willow, unsure if I can trust this guy but really needing his help right now.

"Brodie, can you make sure Willow gets to her car safely?" I ask, and Willow starts to frantically shake her head.

"Of course, man, I got her," he says, and I lift my chin in a silent thank you.

"I don't need him to help me to my car. I can get there by myself; plus, there's plenty of people outside!" Willow argues, knowing she's fighting a losing battle when all three of us shake our heads at her.

"Willow, please. It will make me feel better knowing you got to your car safely," Aly pleads with her. "We would take you ourselves if we didn't have to get Sosie home right away."

Willow's eyes narrow on Aly, and then she looks at Sosie and huffs. "Fine." She turns to Brodie, pointing her finger at him. "If you say or do anything to piss me off, I will put my heel so far into your foot that you'll never be able to wear skates again."

Brodie's lips twitch as he brings his hand to his forehead and salutes her as if she's his commanding officer. If I wasn't so concerned about Sosie, I would laugh. Maybe Aly was right about the two of them being perfect for each other.

We say goodbye to both of them and walk Sosie out of the bar. She can barely keep her head up, and walking with her is nearly impossible. We are almost to the car when all of a sudden she stops and jerks her head up.

"I'm going to throw up," she says, and I drop her arm as if she just burned me. Aly is the sensible one between us, and she turns her away from us so she can throw up near the building we're next to. She holds Sosie's hair and rubs her back, softly reassuring her that everything's going to be okay.

"Gavin, we can see the car from here. Go run and bring it to us, please," Aly tells me while Sosie continues to upchuck.

"I'm not leaving you alone."

"Gavin, you can see us the whole time. She's going to be useless once she's done. Go now!" Aly demands, and I realize she's right.

I run to my truck, get in, and turn it on. Aly was right; I can see them the whole time, and within seconds, I pull up beside them. Aly is holding Sosie against her, using the wall as her support system.

"Is she done?" I ask after I get out of the truck and open the back door.

"Yes, help me get her in the back seat."

I bend down and scoop Sosie up, carrying her to my truck. I place her as gently as I can, laying her down across the leather bench.

"Do you have a plastic bag?" Aly asks, and

I open the passenger door to get a bag out of the pocket in my door. I hand it to Aly, who grabs hold of the handrail and hoists herself up into the back to be with Sosie.

"What are you doing?" I ask, not liking the fact that she's not going to sit up front with me.

"I'm going to sit back here with her. If she needs to throw up while you're driving, I can hold the bag for her."

"No."

"No?" She shakes her head.

"She's not buckled in, which means you can't be either."

"Can you please not act crazy right now? I'll be fine. Just drive carefully." Seeing she's not going to give in, I place a swift kiss on her lips. "You're really amazing to want to help her out, especially after the way she's treated you."

She just shrugs and looks once more at Sosie before returning her eyes to me. "I know if the roles were reversed, I would appreciate someone helping me out." She swings her legs in, and I close the door after her. I walk around to my side of the truck and open the door to get in. "You do realize it's probably going to be a long night, right?"

I look at my girl through the rearview mirror and grimace. All my plans to do very naughty things to her are now down the drain. "Yeah, I know," I grumble, pissed off at Sosie for ruining the ending to my amazing evening. I reverse the car out of my parking spot and hear Sosie moan when I hit the brakes to put the car in Drive. An evil smile forms on my face when I think of how wicked her hangover is going to be tomorrow.

Payback's a bitch!

Fifteen

GAVIN

$\mathcal{I}$ STARE DOWN at the numbers the marketing department just slid in front of me, a slew of emotions internally running wild as I look at them in shock. Never in my wildest dreams did I think so many people would preorder my first album. I'm speechless, humbled, and damn fucking proud.

The last couple weeks have felt like a dream, with things going so well both personally and professionally. We released the cover of the album the same day the second track came out called "My Ride or Die." The song climbed straight to the top of the country music charts and made its debut in the top twenty of the Billboard charts.

"For a new artist, these numbers are extraordinary. We're very happy, Gavin, and we hope you are too," Atticus Langston tells me, everyone around the table nodding in agreement with him. It's very rare for Atticus to attend these types of meetings, so the air is thick with tension from his presence.

"I'm beyond happy and grateful," I say, nodding at Atticus. "Thank you," I tell everyone, looking around the table. "I'm so thankful for you all and your hard work. Because of everyone, release day is going to be amazing."

The album drops in three weeks, and it seems unreal that we're finally so close. The conversation turns to discussing our schedule for publicity during the album's release. Some of it requires out-of-town travel, and I make a mental note to ask Aly if she can get off work to join me for even part of it. A couple more pressing items are discussed and then the meeting wraps up, and everyone, including me, stands up to leave the conference room.

"Gavin, do you mind sticking around for a

minute?" Atticus asks.

"Of course." I sit back down and plaster a smile on my face, wondering why he wants to speak with me privately. When the last person shuts the door behind them, Atticus turns back toward me and smiles.

"Now that it's just you and me, we can cut all the bullshit and be honest. Are you really happy at Charisma Records?" His smile is just as phony as he is, because I know he doesn't care about my happiness. All he cares about is if he can make a profit off me and my music. Record companies shell out a lot of money on their artists, so I know the bottom line is all that matters to a man like Atticus Langston.

"I don't bullshit people, Mr. Langston. If I had any issues, they would've been discussed already." I look him straight in the eye so he can see I'm serious. "What's the reasoning behind this question?"

"No reason, other than the fact that you've been spotted out publicly at numerous functions held by another record label. The rumor mill amongst our peers is beginning to turn. That is not the type of negative attention I want brought upon us."

"If you're referring to functions hosted by Big Little Music, then that's only because my girlfriend works for them." I grit my teeth in frustration, since he damn well knows the reasoning. It has only been a handful of outings, most of them not public, so who the fuck is telling him this shit?

"Ah, so you're serious about the girl?" He gives me a doubtful look, and my hand fists in anger underneath the table.

Fuck, I hated this guy when I was dating his daughter… and I still hate him now.

"Her name is Alyson, and I've been serious about her from the moment I met her."

He stares at me a moment longer before looking down and folding his hands. "I trust you, Gavin, because I know how appreciative you are for everything we've done for you. However, I don't trust Kathleen Davidson. I have no doubt she's plotting to try to steal you from us when your contract is up."

"Well, then, I guess you'll just have to make me an offer I can't refuse." I smile coldly at him and mimic his movements by folding my hands in front of me. Kathleen Davidson hasn't said one word to me about joining Big Little

Music. She's been nothing but gracious and kind every time I've seen her. If I'm honest, I've enjoyed seeing how much she values her employees with the amount of employee appreciation functions she hosts, and since there were other spouses and partners at these events, it never seemed odd for me to attend with Aly.

Now that I think about this, the only thing that ever seemed odd is Aly's reaction to Kathleen. She completely shuts down and barely looks at her when she's approached us. When she does acknowledge Kathleen, her expression always holds a touch of wariness. I need to remember to ask Aly what's up between them.

"We'll worry about that when the time comes. All depends on sales, right?" He raises an eyebrow at me, and I agree with a nod. "Now, onto some other business. I want to rehire you to write for Tori."

I chuckle softly, not believing how big this man's balls really are. "I don't think that's a good idea, Mr. Langston."

He knows his daughter cheated behind my back. Seemed everyone knew except for me. The worst part about it all is that she won't even admit to her wrongdoings and instead, she's acted like the victim. Two weeks ago, she made the nominee luncheon almost unbearable. I would've walked out if it weren't for Aly, who was bearing the brunt of it all. Thank God for Aly's boss, Shane, who found more chairs to cram around the Big Little Music table for us to sit there during the event. I didn't give a fuck about what people were saying that night. All I cared about was Aly and her feelings. She was more upset that Tori was ruining my big moment than she was about how Tori was treating her.

"She'll behave herself, Gavin. I'll make sure of it."

"I'm sorry, but no," I tell him firmly, trying to still sound respectful when all I feel is disgust for him right now.

"The lease on your apartment is just about up. How about we sign a new lease and I'll pay for the next year upfront?"

I can see the steel look of determination in his eyes, and it makes me more than ready to fight back.

"Thank you, but I'm currently looking for

a new place to live. Something bigger." That's only half-true. I want to get out of my place, because I don't want him to have anything else over my head. I've practically moved in with Aly since the night of the hockey game. While I like her place a lot, I would prefer us to find something more secure and bigger. Something we can call "ours" together.

"We can move you into one of the penthouses. I personally know there's one vacant right now."

I shake my head at him. "No, thank you."

"I'll pay you fifty thousand dollars on top of your normal rate and royalties."

My jaw clenches in anger that this man thinks I have no morals or respect for my girlfriend by accepting his bribes.

"The answer is still fucking no," I growl and push back from the table, tired of this conversation. Placing both my fists on the table, I lean into it so he can see I'm not playing his games. "I can't be bought, Atticus."

"Everyone can be bought, Gavin." He slithers out of his chair and stands. "Don't make any rash decisions right now. Sleep on it—you have too much at stake to make the wrong decision."

What the fuck does that mean? "Are you threatening me?"

"I look forward to hearing from you soon, Gavin." He doesn't respond to my question and instead turns around and walks out of the conference room.

Right then and there, I know this will be the only album I ever make with Charisma records.

♡♡♡♡♡♡

"HE'S GOT YOU by the balls, man," Scotty Wilkins says with a shake of his head. He knew as soon as I walked into the studio that something was wrong by my demeanor, and I couldn't help but vent to him about it, since he knows firsthand exactly what happens behind closed doors in this industry.

"Do you really think so? I've built up a solid reputation as a songwriter without him," I point out, since I've been in Nashville longer than I've been signed with Charisma.

"True, but look at his catalog of musicians. He's got some big ones."

"I don't need him to land a big fish. Been

there, done that already." My hard work, talent, and reputation got me working with a couple of big names in country music. Word of mouth is still the number-one best way of getting your name out there.

"Atticus Langston still runs this town and until you're just as powerful as he is, I wouldn't piss him off." He shakes his head. "I would take his offer and just make sure you always have other people in the room with you and Tori."

"I need to talk to Aly first. I'm not taking the job without her blessing." I will not jeopardize my relationship for money. If Aly doesn't want me to accept it, then I won't do it. "Even if Aly says yes, I still don't like the idea of being in the same room with Tori, let alone having to work with her again."

"It's just business, Gavin. Leave the past in the past and just act professional."

I know Scotty's right and I can be professional while working with Tori, but her behavior has proved she's not to be trusted.

"How do you like being with Big Little Music?" I ask out of curiosity. I've only heard good things so far from other artists, but I know Scotty would tell me straight his honest opinion about them.

"They've been very good to me, but I would count them out if you're thinking about signing with them after your contract with Charisma is up."

"Why?"

"Because they have a very strict policy of no interoffice dating, which includes the talent."

My eyebrows shoot up in surprise that he even knows about this rule. "I'm shocked you actually read the employee manual," I tease, because I still haven't read the rules at Charisma yet. Scotty doesn't seem the type to follow the rules anyway.

"I didn't. I slept with one of the assistants and she got fired. So yeah, they take that shit seriously over there."

"Ouch. You're a fucking asshole."

"I did feel like an asshole. Fortunately, she was able to get another job right away."

"Do you think that rule would apply to Aly and me? If I ever did sign with Big Little Music, that is."

He thinks about it for a few moments before

answering. "It might not since you would have an established relationship already. They wouldn't assign her to you though, since that would be a conflict of interest."

"Yeah, you're probably right." The more I think about it, the more I love the idea of working with Aly. But Scotty is right - they wouldn't put us together.

"Don't sweat this shit, Gavin. Why don't you ask Aly about it?"

"I don't want to bring it up to her just yet. If this record does well, Charisma might want to sign me for another three records." With the preorder sales what they were, I would be shocked if Charisma didn't want to renew my contract.

"I thought you were done working with them?" he asks with a confused expression on his face.

"I would like to be, but what if it's an offer I would be crazy to refuse? At the end of the day, we all want to make money and be able to take care of our families." I doubt they'll offer me another contract, but you never know what might happen.

"Then you should take it but what's the

difference between them giving you another contract and taking Atticus's money to write for Tori again? That's a crazy offer for you to refuse." *Shit, he has a point.* "Either way, you're still dancing with the devil," he says with a smug smile on his face.

I hate it when he's right.

I glance at my watch to see we've been gossiping like girls for almost an hour now. "We need to get back to writing so I'm not late for my date with Aly tonight."

He nods in agreement and picks up his acoustic guitar. "Ok, but here's my last piece of advice. Talk to Aly, but I highly recommend you take that offer."

"I'll think about it some more," I tell him before we continue where we left off with the song we were working on.

Sixteen

ALY

"*T*HIS HAS BEEN the best lunch break I've ever had in my life," I say in a lazy voice, completely satiated from the intense orgasm Gavin just gave me. The circles he's drawing on my back with his fingers are lulling me to sleep like a lullaby, and I groan, hating the idea of having to get up soon. "I wish we didn't have to go back to work."

"Me too, baby, but just think—as soon as you agree to move in with me, we can do this every day for the rest of our lives." He kisses me deeply, sending shivers down my spine at the thought of this being my forever.

We've been together for over a month now, and every day with him still feels like a dream. Even things with Sosie have changed for the better. After I took care of her the night she got drunk, she's done a complete one-eighty with me. She even apologized to me the next day when we took her to brunch. I didn't do what I did to gain her approval, but I have to admit it felt good for her to let me in.

My eyes slide closed thinking about the pain I heard in her voice when she told me that besides Gavin and his family, what I did for her was one of the nicest things anyone had ever done for her. She told me she couldn't believe I still took care of her after she'd been a huge bitch. I was honestly surprised when she started to cry, saying I had proven that I loved Gavin and I didn't deserve her lashing out at me. I thought it might have been lack of sleep and a hangover that made her apologize for her past behavior, especially when she asked if we could be friends, but since then, we've grabbed a bite to eat together a couple times without Gavin, and she came out shopping once with me and Valerie. I wouldn't say we're close, but I have hope that one day we might be.

"I didn't say I wouldn't move in with you, babe. I said we're in no rush. You practically live here anyway." I huff at him, trying to stay focused on my point while he trails kisses down my neck.

He rolls me over, and my legs immediately spread for him. He settles in between them and stares at me. "Promise me that we'll start looking for a place when we get back from California." It isn't a question, but more like a demand as he gazes into my eyes.

"I promise," I whisper, a lump of emotion wedging into my throat as I get lost in him. I have an overwhelming urge to tell him I love him. To tell him he's my everything. No one has ever made me feel as beautiful, as loved, as secure and protected as he does. In such a short amount of time, this man has become my whole world.

I can't imagine one single day without him in it, and even though I've given myself freely to him, a tiny, minuscule part of me is still scared. It's that part of me that prevents me from saying those three big words he's longing to hear from me.

What are you waiting for, Aly? Tell him!

I gulp down my emotions, and before I can utter the words, the alarm on my phone goes off, indicating my lunch break is over.

"Let's get you ready for work, darlin'." He lifts himself off me and just like that, the moment is over.

Disappointment swirls within me, and I silently yell at myself for being such a coward. I slowly sit up and watch him get dressed until that magnificent body of his is covered. I swing my legs over the side of the bed and get up to use the restroom.

"Have you seen my phone? I need to call Sosie and tell her to meet me at my apartment later." We look around my room but don't see it.

"You probably left it in your car. Here, just use mine to text her. I need to freshen up before I get dressed." I hand him my phone before going into the bathroom. I quickly wash myself with soap and warm water, dry off, apply lotion, and brush my teeth. I wrap myself in my robe and go back into my room. I stop dead in my tracks when I see the look on Gavin's face as he stares at my phone.

"What's wrong, what happened?" I rush toward him and grab his forearm, but he shakes my hand off him.

"What the fuck is this, Aly?" he asks in a calm, deadly voice. His eyes are anything but calm when he looks at me and raises my phone for me to see the screen. I read the text displayed, and my breath gets caught in my throat while my stomach starts to hurt from reading the words.

Kathleen Davidson: I had lunch with Scotty today. He told me Gavin has been inquiring about BLM. Great job! Keep your eyes on the prize and that promotion will soon be yours.

My hands ball into fists, and I look up at the man I love, seeing betrayal in his eyes. "I know this looks bad, but it's not what it seems," I say while he stares at me as if I'm a complete stranger.

"It's not? Then what the hell is it? Because it seems pretty crystal-fucking-clear that once again I'm being used by someone I care about," he growls, looking at me the same way he looks at Tori, his eyes starting to fill with hatred.

"I can explain, baby." I hold up my hands, trying to explain to keep him from walking out. "Kathleen approached me a couple weeks ago, asking me if you were happy at Charisma. I told her that we don't talk about business, and that's when she offered me a promotion if I tried to convince you to sign with us once your contract is done."

Without a word, he sidesteps around me and stomps down the stairs. His strides are so long that I have to run to keep up with him, my grip on the railing is the only thing preventing me from falling down.

"Gavin, I told her no!" I reach the bottom of the stairs and run past him to block him from walking out the front door. "Did you hear me? I told her no!"

The emotions playing on his face are telling me he's barely listening to me, too deep in his own thoughts to hear the truth.

"Why didn't you tell me when that happened?" he asks in a dangerous voice, his eyes narrowed in doubt.

"I didn't tell you, because I didn't want you to doubt my feelings for you. We are so new. And considering your past relationship,

I knew you might not believe me." My throat gets tight. "I didn't think this would ever come up again because I told her no!" I say quickly, my voice rising and my eyes begging him to trust me. "I know that was wrong and I should've told you right away. I'm sorry, Gavin! Please… you've got to believe me!"

He stares at me, his eyes searching mine to see if I'm telling the truth. "How do I know you're telling the truth? You could be playing me just like I've been played before."

"No!" I cry out, tears starting to stream down my cheeks. "I would *never* do that to you. I'm not Tori. I love you!"

He laughs, the sound cruel and mocking, cutting my heart open. "The words I've been waiting to hear from you, and this is the time you decide to tell me? Like I would fucking believe them right now?"

"But it's true. I do, Gavin. I do love you!" I shake my head at him, not believing this is happening. I feel like my world is crumbling down around me.

"Move away from the door," he growls, refusing to look at me, and any remnants of hope I have start to fade away.

"No," I whisper, and instead, I throw myself at him, wrapping my arms around his waist tightly and locking my hands together, because I'm not letting him go. I can't. "Gavin. Please… you have to trust me." The thought of losing him breaks the dam of tears, my shoulders rocking hard as I bawl into his chest. Wetness soaks the front of his shirt, and we just stand there for a moment, the sounds of my anguish filling the air. Minutes pass, and I finally feel him touch me, his hands gently gripping my biceps as he tries to lean back.

"I need some time to think, Aly," he says in a tone that has me lifting my head up to look at him. I know I probably look like a mess, but I don't care. I blink to clear my vision and search his eyes, noticing his expression isn't as hard as before but still missing that special look he has only for me. The one filled with warmth and love.

God, I'm such an idiot. But he's being an idiot too! He should know what we have and trust me.

"I need to be alone to think. Let me go," he says gently, reaching behind his back to pry my hands apart. Tears start to spring to my eyes again, and all I can do is shake my head at him. "I'll call you later when I'm ready to talk."

"Do you promise?" I croak out, my throat raw from crying. "You need to trust me," I repeat again, looking him in the eye.

"I'll call you."

A lone tear falls down my cheek, and he reaches up to wipe it away with the pad of his thumb. I exhale the breath I was holding and nod, releasing my hands and dropping my arms from around him, feeling defeated. I hate letting him go, but I know there's nothing I can do but wait.

He walks around me, and I turn to watch him go, wanting so badly to yell and scream at him that he's making the wrong choice. Another wave of tears starts to fall. He stops and takes one more look at me before closing the door behind him. I shuffle over to my window and watch him run a hand through his hair as he walks away. I stand there until I see his truck drive by, and it's only then I run upstairs and throw myself onto my bed to cry.

I allow myself a few minutes to wallow in self-pity, and then I tell myself to stop crying.

There's no way I can go into work looking like this, so I text Shane, telling him I need to take the rest of the afternoon off. He doesn't text back right away, so I call Valerie, but she doesn't pick up. I then try calling Willow, but she doesn't answer her cell phone either. I call Willow's office, and the receptionist tells me she's on her lunch break. Willow always goes home on her lunch break, so I quickly get dressed, text her that I'm coming to see her, and drive to her house.

She still hasn't texted me back by the time I get to her house across town, but her car is in her driveway. I park behind another car in front of her house and walk up to the front porch. I start banging on her door, needing her to open it right away, as the tears start flowing and I'm about to lose it.

She finally pulls the door open, her face contorted into anger until she sees me in my crying state. "Oh my God, Aly, what's wrong?" she asks in a panic, grabbing my wrist and hauling me inside. She closes the doors and pulls me in for a hug.

"It's Gavin," I cry into her neck, my sobs preventing me from speaking coherently.

"He's... going... to... break... up... with... me," I stutter out, the weight of those words causing me to cry harder.

She holds me tighter and in a soothing voice tells me it's going to be okay. I take a couple minutes to collect myself before pulling back out of her embrace.

"I'm so sorry, Willow, for snotting all over you. I—" My voice falters as I take in her appearance. She's wearing only a baggy, navy-blue T-shirt, with the hem of the shirt stopping at the middle of her bare thighs.

I look her up and down in confusion, wondering why she's dressed like this on her lunch break then bringing my gaze back to her face. "Are you sick?" I watch her gulp and her eyes focus behind me. I turn around, my eyes widening in shock to see Brodie Larsen, gloriously half-naked with disheveled hair and jeans hanging low on his hips, standing in her bedroom doorway.

"Hey, Al," he says softly with a tentative smile. "You okay?"

I inhale sharply and whip my head back to look at my best friend. Her lips are swollen, hair disheveled as well, and her cheeks are turning crimson under my scrutiny.

"You have a lot of explaining to do, Mayson." I exhale the breath I was holding. "You told me the night I introduced you two that he was a conceited asshole." I narrow my eyes at her in questioning.

"He can be," she answers with a twitch of her lips and looks at him with adoration. I hear his chuckling getting closer and then he's standing next to her, his arm around her waist.

"I'm so confused right now," I grumble with a shake of my head. "How long has this been going on?"

"Since that same night I told you he was a conceited asshole." She looks at me sheepishly, knowing she's in so much trouble.

"What the hell, you guys!" I yell out in anger, throwing my arms up and placing them on my hips. "You haven't said one word about this, Willow!"

"I know, and I'm sorry. I've kind of just been wrapped up in Brodie." He kisses her forehead tenderly, and she looks at him in a way I've never seen her look at any other man before. She looks at him like she's in love with him—the complete opposite of what her feelings were over a month ago. "Just like you've been preoccupied with Gavin."

At the mere mention of his name, tears spring up again and I look up, willing them not to fall. "Yeah, well, that's about to change."

"Aly, do I need to go punch his face in?" Brodie's demeanor changes, his eyes glittering with anger. "Because it would be my pleasure if he's hurt you."

I shake my head at him and give him a sad smile. "No. This is actually my fault, but thank you for looking out for me."

"I'll give you two some privacy to talk." He looks down at Willow and smirks, his eyes darkening as he rakes his eyes up and down her body. "Even though my shirt looks sexy as fuck on you, babe, I'm going to need it back unless you want me to walk out of here shirtless."

"Be right back, Aly. Make yourself at home."

They go into the bedroom, and I busy myself in the kitchen, grabbing a cup of water to distract myself from hearing their whispers and kisses. Willow comes out of the bedroom in her work clothes, with Brodie right behind her. He gives me a tight hug then kisses Willow goodbye, promising her they will see each other later before he leaves.

"I called work and told them I'm taking the rest of the day off. So sit down and tell me everything."

We sit down on her couch, and I start from the very beginning of when Kathleen first approached me to her text message today.

"You should've told him, Aly," she says softly after I finished my story.

"Yeah, I know." I nod sadly in agreement. "I had no idea he was talking to Scotty about Big Little Music. I knew he was upset about having to work with Tori again, and I told him I didn't care and that I trusted him, but that was the extent of our talks about him being unhappy at Charisma." Gavin told me about Atticus's threat and offer to write for Tori again. I wasn't happy about it, but I told him to do it for his career. After reassuring him that I trusted him and I wasn't going to be upset with him having to work with her, I haven't thought about it again. I've put off worrying about it, because they aren't supposed to start working on her new album for another couple weeks.

"Well, you can't undo the past," she says with a sigh. "And I don't think he's going to break up with you. He loves you."

I shrug, not really knowing how to respond to that. "I know he loves me but—" I let out a shaky breath. "—the look in his eyes, Willow..." I shiver thinking about it. "He looked like he hated me." I know after I refused to let him go and cried, something softened in his eyes, but I still don't know where his head's at. "He said he needed time to think, and I knew I had to let him go." I look down and pick at another one of my nails, noticing I've chipped the nail polish off most of them in my despair.

"He probably just needs some time to think things through. I've seen the way that man looks at you. He isn't breaking up with you," she says confidently while studying me closely. "Do you really love him, Aly?"

"With every fiber of my being," I tell her firmly, my eyes unwavering as I look at her so she knows I'm serious. "But I'm mad at him too."

"What do you mean?"

"He should trust me. I know he was mad, but he should have known I wouldn't do something like that to him."

"You're right," she agrees then looks down and takes a shaky breath before bringing her gaze back up to mine. "That said, you know his history and you knew that not telling him and him finding out about Kathleen might cause problems."

"Yeah." I swallow hard, seeing only one solution to this problem. "I need to quit my job."

"What?" Her eyes widen as I start to come up with a plan to prove to Gavin he's what really matters to me. Handing in my notice should prove to him that I'm with him for only him and not advancement in the music industry. "I'll quit my job and get a job somewhere else."

"Do you really want to quit your job?"

"No, I mean I love my job, but I'm not happy Kathleen put me in this situation. And I can apply what I do to almost any industry, so I'm not worried about finding work."

"You're talented and smart, so I know you're right. If you're sure about this, then I can help you reconstruct your resume." She takes my hands as I smile in my excitement of finding a solution. I hug her, tackling her to her couch.

"I love you so much, Willow Mayson!" I say to her as I squeeze her to me. "Thank you for always being here for me."

"I love you too, Aly." She returns my hug, her arms tightening around me. I pull back so she can stand up. "Now get in that car, call Shane to give him your notice, and go find Gavin!"

"I will, but you have to know that when this drama is over, we're going to have a conversation about you and Brodie."

"I figured as much." She rolls her eyes.

I give her a hug goodbye then race out of her house. Hope starts to fill me as I get into my car, shut the door, and start the engine. *Please, God, this has to work!* I have enough savings in the bank to live comfortably for six months until I find my next job. And while I'll miss Shane and some of my co-workers, Kathleen showing her true colors makes me second-guess if Big Little Music is where I'm meant to be. I dial Shane's number, praying he picks up and understands when I tell him why I'm quitting.

"Baby girl, you should've told me," he says sadly after I finish. We've been talking for the whole thirty minutes I've been stuck in traffic, and I'm now parked across the street from Gavin's building. I have no idea if he's home, since he normally parks in his building's garage, but I figured I can start here first and then go hunt him down at the studio.

"I should've told a lot of people, and now I'm paying the price for it."

"I'm so fucking livid right now, Alyson!" I've never heard Shane this angry in my life, but with Kathleen owning the company, there isn't much he can do if he wants to keep his job. "You shouldn't be in this kind of position."

"But I am, Shane. Do you understand why I'm quitting though? Even if Gavin and I aren't together any longer, there's no way I can continue working there for her."

"I completely understand, but you know I'm connected in this industry. I can get you another job at another label like *that*." I hear his fingers snap and smile in sadness, as I truly will miss working for him, but I know he's my friend for life.

"I think it's best that I choose another industry, no matter what the outcome of my relationship with Gavin will be." The more I think about it, the more it makes sense for me to completely get out of the music industry. I couldn't bear to stay in it anyway if he and I don't end up together, knowing I might see him with other women at industry events. The image of him even holding hands with someone else makes bile rise up in my throat.

"I need to give Kathleen a piece of my mind right now when I tell her the news of your resignation. I love you, my sunshine. Call me after you find Gavin to let me know what's happened. If you need me, I'm here."

I say goodbye and hang up with him. I look over at Gavin's building and take a deep breath. *Please let him be home*, I pray as I get out of my car and walk across the street. I type my code into the keypad and open the door when the buzzer sounds.

"Good afternoon, Miss Dawson," the doorman says to me on my way in. I nod and smile in greeting, too nervous to even talk right now. I punch the up button and the elevator doors slide open. I smooth down my hair, pinch my cheeks for some color, and wipe the corners of my eyes while the elevator rises to Gavin's floor. I take a shaky breath when the doors open and lift my head up in confidence as I walk out, determined to win my man back. This is our first major bump in our journey together, and I know we can overcome it.

I stand in front of his door, praying he's home so I don't have to go searching for him. I knock rapidly, and it takes only a few seconds for the door to open. Time seems to stand still as Tori Langston stands before me in only her green lace bra and matching panties.

"Wh… what are you doing here?" I whisper as I blink back the tears that are threatening to spill.

She smiles like the Cheshire Cat and folds her arms beneath her chest, causing her boobs to almost spill out of her bra. "You know exactly what I've been doing here, sweet little Alyson."

"Where's Gavin?" I look around her, my vision blurring as I see her clothes littering the floor, making a trail around the corner to where his bedroom is.

"He's taking a shower," she purrs and bites her lip, making me want to throw up all over her.

"He wouldn't." I shake my head at her, not believing he would throw away what we have and return to this vile woman.

"It was just a matter of time that he and I were going to be back together. Did you really think he was going to settle for a little girl when he can have a real woman?" She snickers as she looks me up and down in disgust. Tiny knives start puncturing my heart, my body shaking in anger, hurt, and betrayal. My chest feels like it's about to explode, and I can't stand to look at her anymore. Without saying a word, I bolt for the nearest exit and run down the stairs.

"*No, no, no!*" I scream in the stairwell, not caring if anyone hears me. I finally reach the first floor and pull open the door. I run through the lobby to the glass doors, ignoring the doorman, who calls after me in concern. I get outside and run across the street to my car, horns blaring, as I don't even watch where I'm going and almost get hit by a car. I reach my car and fumble in my purse for my keys but can't find them through the tears that are blocking my vision.

"Aly? *Aly*, are you okay?" I hear Sosie's voice and look up to see her running toward me. I yank open my door and shut it just as she arrives. "Aly, what's going on? *Aly!* Roll down your window and talk to me," she pleads with me while banging on the window.

I start the engine and roll down the window, gasping for air as I try to breathe through my heartache. "Gavin… and… Tori," I stutter out before a fresh wave of tears assaults me.

"What? No!" Understanding enters her eyes and she shakes her head in denial. "He wouldn't!" she says in disbelief.

"Looks like he did," I whisper, my heart in agony at how much this hurts. Needing solitude, I roll up my window and briefly glance up to see Sosie running toward Gavin's building. Feeling numb, I put the car in reverse, back out, and get the hell out of there.

Seventeen

GAVIN

I CLOSE MY eyes and tilt my head back, the lukewarm water from the shower washing over me. I've been in here for a while, replaying what transpired with Aly over and over in my head. After I left her house, I mindlessly drove around town until I came back here and decided a shower might help clear my mind.

Seeing her cry and beg me to trust her shredded my heart, and I keep trying to think what I would've done if I were in her shoes. I would've fucking said something right away, but I've come to understand Aly's point of why she didn't tell me at first. From the beginning,

Aly has been interested in getting to know me as a person, not Gavin McNeer, the country music singer, and her actions have always proven that. She's never inserted herself into my career and has always been supportive. When I need her, she's there for me. It has always been me who would talk business, not her. Since day one, Aly's been with me for the right reasons.

"Shit," I mumble, realizing I've completely fucked up. I stretch my arms out in front of me against the tile wall of the shower and hang my head down, trying to come up with a plan to prove to her that I do trust her.

Once I'm done with my shower, I'll call Aly and see if she can meet me. I need to reassure her that we're going to be okay. This is our first argument, and I'm sure it won't be our last, but what I do know is I won't let this break us. Even though this situation is going to make seeing Kathleen Davidson very awkward from now on, but I'll do it for Aly.

I'm so deep in my thoughts that I don't hear the shower door open. Hands wrap around me from behind, startling me. I feel a cheek against my back and assume it's Aly, since only she and Sosie have a key to my apartment. I sigh in relief, grateful she's sought me out.

"Baby, I'm so glad you're here," I tell her with a smile, feeling her hands slowly moving down my abs, making their way to my cock. I look down at those hands and pause, my smile fading in confusion.

Aly never paints her nails red.

I turn around and my jaw drops open in shock when I see Tori standing there and not Aly.

"What the hell do you think you're doing?" I roar in fury, my vision going red in anger. I feel like I need another shower to wash off the poison from her touch. "Get the fuck out of here!" I twist the shower knob off with one hand, and with my other, wrap it around her bicep and walk her out of the shower. I grab a towel and wrap it around my waist, not offering her one as I walk into my bedroom to grab my cell phone to call the police. I look at my screen to see I have two missed calls from Sosie and one from Aly. *Fuck!*

"Awe, sweetie, why are you acting this way? You know you've missed me." She tries to reach for me, but I sidestep around her and start picking up her clothes that she's left all over my floor. I follow the trail into the living room, and once they're all picked up, I push them into her arms.

"Get dressed and get the fuck out. How did you get into my apartment?" I question with narrowed eyes. I had my locks changed after we broke up in case this kind of shit happened.

"Money will buy you everything, Gavin."

I look at her in disgust, seeing she's exactly like her father, and it makes me realize I don't want to be associated with these two anymore.

"It will never buy me! I'm filing a restraining order against your psycho ass." I watch her throw back her head and laugh, as if I just told her the funniest shit she's ever heard.

What in the hell did I ever see in her?

"Go ahead, if you want to watch your career go down the drain," she threatens with a crazy glint in her eye. She walks over to my couch and sits down to start putting her clothes on.

I need to burn that couch.

I turn to go to my bedroom to get dressed, when I stop dead in my tracks at the sound of a key sliding into my lock.

Fuck, that better not be Aly!

I say a silent prayer of thanks when the door is thrown open and Sosie barrels in. She stops short and looks between me and Tori, her face crestfallen as she sees our unclothed bodies. I grip the towel around my waist tighter while Tori takes her time putting her clothes back on.

"Gavin, how could you?" she cries out in anguish, tears looking like they're pooling in her eyes.

"How could I what? I didn't do anything! This bitch broke into my place while I was taking a shower." Sosie looks over at Tori, who smirks at her in confirmation. "I was just about to get dressed to go down to the police station."

"You're committing career suicide, Gavin," Tori warns while hooking her bra back on. She seems calm right now, but I can see her hands shaking.

"My career was just fine before I met you. If anything, being associated with you has probably tarnished it."

She shakes her head at me and continues to get dressed. Tori's reputation in the industry is at an all-time low, making me wonder how many of my peers were actually laughing behind my back when I was dating her.

"If nothing happened, then why does Aly think something did?"

My head whips around back to Sosie, panic starting to fill me at what she's implying. "When did you see Aly?"

"I just saw her downstairs a couple minutes ago, bawling her eyes out. She told me you two were together. Why would she think that?" Sosie and I stare at each other before we both look over at Tori, whose evil smile confirms she's behind Aly thinking we slept together.

"What the fuck did you say to her?" I slowly move toward her, ready to haul her ass out of here, but not before she tells me what she did.

She stands up from the couch and slips her feet into her high heels. "I didn't want to be rude and let your guest think you weren't home, so I opened the door and told her you were in the shower. I can't help she assumed we slept together when she saw I was only wearing my bra and underwear." The smug look of satisfaction on her face causes me to stop thinking rationally. I rush toward her and grip her arms hard, wanting to shake that fucking look off her face.

"If one bruise is noticeable on me, I will tell everyone you assaulted me in the shower." As if her words were fire to my skin, I let her go, choosing to not waste my time on her any longer.

"You think anyone would believe you?" I snort at her and enjoy seeing her smile falter. "Your word doesn't mean shit in this industry anymore. You've tainted everyone and everything you've touched. Your fans will soon follow." I mentally count to ten while I walk to the door and open it for her to leave. "I'm done with you and your father. Find yourself another songwriter. Now get the fuck out of here." I smile coldly at her, despite my temper being held together by a very thin thread.

She walks up to me and has the audacity to caress my cheek before saying, "See you around, lover," and walks out. I slam the door after her, wrap my hands around the back of my neck, and look up at the ceiling to gain my composure.

"That girl is straight up delusional," Sosie says softly after we stand there in silence for a few moments.

I inhale deeply and close my eyes, wishing that today was just a bad dream. But it wasn't and my first priority needs to be saving my relationship. I exhale out a shaky breath and start walking to my bedroom to get dressed. "I need to find Aly."

"Maybe you should give her some time. She was in pretty bad shape when I saw her." Sosie follows me into my room and sits on my bed while I get dressed inside my walk-in closet.

"In this situation, time will only make things worse. I just can't believe she would think I would cheat on her like that." I shake my head at the thought, not understanding why she would for one second think I would not only cheat on her, but go back to someone as despicable as Tori. Then again, I thought she was only with me for a promotion. Fuck!

"Let's play role reversal for a second, Gavin. How would you feel if right after a fight with her, you show up on her doorstep and a hot, half-naked man, who happens to be her ex-boyfriend, answers the door and tells you she's in the shower?" She raises a questioning eyebrow at me, knowing full well how I would react.

I would punch his fucking lights out and never talk to her again, assuming the worst.

"You're right. Thanks for the reality check, Sos."

"You're welcome—that's my job."

I can't help the chuckle that escapes me, because she's the queen at making sure I eat my slice of humble pie and admit when I'm wrong.

"Where do you plan on starting your search for her?" she asks while I finish getting ready. "I doubt she went back to work."

"If she isn't at home or work, then I don't know where she would be. Maybe Shane knows. She would've had to call in and tell him she's not coming back, and if she didn't, he would've called me asking if I know where she is." I don't want to call Valerie or Willow and worry them in case they don't know what's happening yet. I think Shane would be my best bet to start off with. If I can't get a hold of him, then I will just camp out at her place until she comes home.

"I can call him right now if you want?" Sosie offers, and I can tell she wants to find Aly just as much as I do.

"No, I'll call Shane." I come out of my closet dressed and place a couple suitcases on the bed. I reach for my keys and cell phone off my nightstand and put them in my jeans pockets. "I need you to start packing up my stuff for me while I'm gone. I can't stay here any longer. Once I find Aly, I will call you so you can meet me down at the police station."

Sosie's eyes widen in surprise. "You are seriously going to the police?" she asks in disbelief.

"Abso-fucking-lutely. I'm going to file a report about her breaking into my place and get a restraining order against her."

Sosie gets off the bed, throws her arms around my waist, and squeezes. Hugs are a rare commodity from Sosie, so I take what I can get and hug her back. It only lasts a couple of seconds, and she releases her hold on me.

"I'm proud of you, Gav. It might get ugly with the Langstons, but you're doing the right thing."

"I appreciate that, Sos," I tell her while ruffling her hair, and that annoyed expression of hers that I love comes back on her face. "I refuse to let anyone manipulate me for the good of my career. I know I'll be just fine." I give her a tentative smile and nod toward the bed where the suitcases are. "Thanks in advance for helping me pack. I'll call you as soon as I find Aly."

"Good luck!" she calls after me. I briskly make my way out of the apartment and run to the elevators. As soon as the doors close after me to take me downstairs to the garage, I call Shane.

"You have some nerve calling me, asshole," he growls into the phone, answering my question if he's heard from Aly or not.

"Shane, I didn't sleep with that psychopath! She broke into my house while I was showering. Aly just happened to show up after she did and assumed the worst, which Tori led her to believe." I go straight to the point, not wanting to waste any more time on the discussion of Tori. "I plan on filing a police report and getting a restraining order against her after I find Aly."

"Are you kidding me with this? Actually, this does sound very much like something Tori would do. Ugh, why am I believing this nonsense?" Shane says with an exasperated sigh. "Seriously, this stuff is even too crazy for Jerry Springer!"

"Where's Aly, Shane?" I try not to sound too demanding while I start my car and drive out of the garage, but I'd rather have a clear idea of where I'm going than drive around without a clue.

"I don't know if I want to tell you. She told me the whole story, and yes, she should've told you and me about Kathleen's proposition when it happened, but you should've never believed Aly would use you for her career." I let him chastise me without interruption, because he's right, and I need to hear it come from someone other than Sosie.

"You're right, Shane, and I do believe she would never do that. I handled it poorly, and because I needed time to think, the situation has now gotten worse."

"It sure has! Do you know she quit her job for you? Because I'm still having a hard time dealing with that."

"*What?*" I practically run off the road from the shock of the news. I pull over into an office parking lot to try to calm my racing heart.

Aly quit BLM?

"That's right, you big Texas jerk! She thought quitting her job would prove her loyalty to you. If you would've believed in her when she first told you, none of this shit would've happened!"

Even though he's yelling at me, I'm not listening to a word he's saying as my heart breaks at what I've caused her to do.

"Shane!" I yell back, interrupting his next tirade against me. "Tell me where she fucking is! I need to make this right."

Silence is his response back to me as he contemplates whether to tell me or not.

"You better not make me regret this," he warns before telling me. "She's at Radnor Lake. It's her favorite place to go to decompress from stress."

I smile at how funny fate works, because Radnor Lake is one of my favorite places to go hiking in Nashville, and Aly doesn't even know that about me yet.

"She always parks by the visitor center.

Her favorite bench is off of Lake Trail."

"Thanks for believing me, Shane. It means a lot to me," I tell him sincerely. From what I know of Shane, he's extremely loyal. I have no doubt it was hard for him to tell me where she is.

"Don't make me track you down and kill you," he warns, his tone making me chuckle.

"I promise you I won't." I tell him goodbye and drive straight to Radnor Lake, determined to win my baby back.

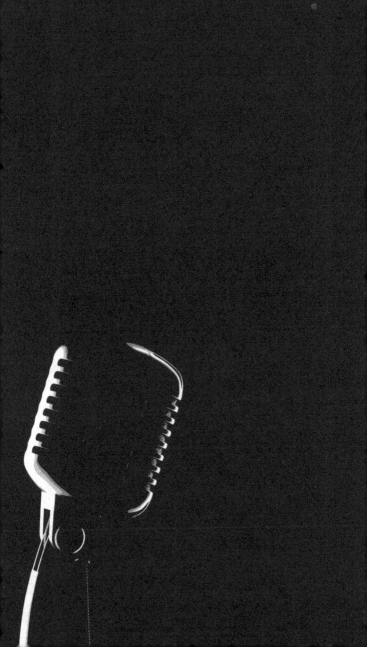

Eighteen

ALY

I SIT ON my favorite bench with my eyes closed, concentrating on my breathing while I listen to the sounds of the glorious nature around me. I count to six as I breathe deeply in and then slowly exhale out, letting my whole body flow with that breath for eight seconds. I open my eyes and take in the most breathtaking view of Radnor Lake.

Not many people know about my love for this park and how I have a special spot here. I've been coming here since I was sixteen, this being the only place I can find refuge in when life turns sad, stressful, or ugly. This bench has absorbed many of my tears, and I deem it my own little sanctuary. Time seems to stand still here, and although I know I haven't been here long, it feels like hours. I shut off my phone after I told Shane what happened and knew I needed peace and quiet. Being here, breathing in the fresh air, and being surrounded by nature helps clear my mind so I can reflect rationally on what transpired today.

After the initial shock of it all wore off, I was able to replay the entire scene back in my head. I technically don't know if Gavin really cheated on me with Tori, since I didn't physically see him. Just because he was taking a shower doesn't mean anything happened between them. Gavin doesn't seem to be the kind of man who goes chasing skirts every time he and his significant other have a fight. Especially getting back together with the person he claims he despises.

He loves you, Aly. You know he wouldn't do that to you, my heart screams at me, but how do you explain Tori being in his apartment?

Gavin's the only one who knows the truth, and there's only one way to find out. I reach into my purse and pull out my phone. I turn the phone back on and take a couple more deep breaths while I wait for it to reboot. I keep the phone on vibrate, so its notifications don't disturb the quietness of nature.

After a couple more moments, I look at my phone to see missed calls and texts messages from Shane and Sosie. At first, I'm disappointed to see there's nothing from Gavin, but then my heart starts to race while reading the missed texts. I smile through tears of happiness as both Shane and Sosie tell me what Tori did and how it was all a misunderstanding.

A new text appears from Shane while I finish reading his old ones.

Shane: Don't be mad at me. He's coming for you, baby girl. I love you!

I would never be mad at Shane for telling Gavin where to find me, because if Shane's willing to give up that information, then that only means he believes Gavin is innocent.

Just like I knew he was.

A calming peace comes over me as I realize everything is going to be okay. This is just a bump in our journey together. We'll have more, but as long as we stick together, we'll always come out stronger.

I sit alone for a little bit longer until I hear the sounds of footsteps coming closer to me. I don't have to look to know it's Gavin, because my body is buzzing with that familiar anticipation. I keep my gaze straight ahead until he's standing before me. He kneels down so that we're eye-to-eye, his hands covering mine, and we stay that way while we stare into each other's souls. I start taking snapshots of him in my mind, hoping to never forget the beauty of this moment with the lake behind him and love radiating from his eyes at me.

"Baby." His voice starts off gruff, and he clears his throat to start over. "Darlin', I'm so sorry about everything that happened today." He starts rubbing his hands over mine, and I briefly close my eyes to bask in their warmth. "I hope you know I would never in a million years disrespect you by being with someone else while we're together. What you saw today was Tori breaking into my apartment and her letting you believe we had sex."

I open my eyes back up to look at him. His eyes pleading with me to accept his apology. I gently place the tips of my fingers over his mouth, not needing him to say another word about it.

"I believe you," I whisper.

He closes his eyes and moans in relief before kissing my fingers. I move my hand away from his mouth and lightly caress his cheeks and jawline. He opens his eyes and leans his head into my hand.

"I know you would never betray me, baby, and I'm sorry for my hotheaded reaction this morning. I promise to work on not letting my past dictate us in the future, but, darlin', you didn't have to quit your job to prove yourself to me."

"You're worth it, Gavin. I would quit it a thousand times over if it eliminates any doubts you have about me." I look tenderly into his eyes and can see how sorry he truly is.

"I have zero doubts about you, Alyson. You're my fucking everything. You've become part of my heartbeat, and knowing I caused you so much pain today has wrecked me."

His words cause my breath to hitch. I grab his face and kiss him with everything I have. "I love you so much, Gavin," I pant in between kisses, his tongue assaulting my senses like it always does.

He looks me in the eyes as he says, "And I love you, Aly." He kisses me one more time and decides to sit down on the bench, demanding I get up to sit on his lap. I sit across his lap, with my legs out in front of me on the bench, and we hold each other while we look out at the lake.

"So, what's next?" I ask after sitting in compatible silence for a while.

He takes a strand of my hair and wraps it behind my ear before kissing the tip of my nose. "We go to the police station to file a report and press charges against Tori. We will also be requesting a restraining order." My eyebrows shoot up in surprise, but I'm beyond happy he's going to take action against her. "Once that's taken care of, we pack up my place and I become a permanent resident of your house." I raise an eyebrow at his bossiness, and he gives me a sheepish smile, with that dimple I so love popping out. "That is, if it's okay with you?"

I kiss his dimple and rest my forehead against his. "What are we waiting for?" I ask with a smile. I get up from his lap and hold out my hand.

He chuckles as he stands up and laces his

fingers through mine. We walk hand in hand back to our cars, ready to start the next chapter of us.

Epilogue

GAVIN

5 months later

I TAKE IN the sea of bodies standing in front of me and marvel at the fact that all these people, from all over the world, are standing in this frigid cold weather on New Year's Eve in Times Square, listening to me sing. With the stage lights in my eyes, I can't see all of them, but I know thousands of them are there, and I want to make sure they have a damn good time.

I look over at Aly to gauge the crowd's reaction, and she's nodding her head at me, giving me a thumbs-up and mouthing *I love you*. She looks stunningly beautiful, her black faux-fur headwrap accentuating her whiskey eyes and porcelain skin, and I can't wait to bring in the New Year with her.

Goddamn, I'm a lucky bastard.

When I got the invitation to perform during the live New Year's Eve broadcast, I decided we needed to spend our holidays together in NYC. We arrived the day before Christmas Eve, doing all the tourist attractions, walking everywhere, shopping, and eating copious amounts of food. Sosie and Valerie joined us for Christmas Eve and Christmas Day then flew home together the following day. I could've had Sosie stay longer, but I wanted alone time with Aly. I know all of our families are back home watching, and tonight is going to be just another monumental night in our adventures together. Life with Aly has been a dream come true, and I thank God every day for bringing me this angel.

This opportunity to sing tonight has just been one of the many doors that have opened my way. When Atticus Langston heard what his daughter had done, he tried to once again buy my silence. Instead, I negotiated for him to let me out of my contract early after the album released and I wouldn't press charges. The restraining order was non-negotiable, and she's not allowed to come within twenty feet of me and Aly. My debut album did so well that I was able to get picked up by another reputable record label and am currently working on my next album for them. An album that is filled with songs inspired by Aly.

Aly being out of a job was the perfect opportunity for her to become my manager. She refused the job at first, but with much convincing and multiple orgasms within a forty-eight-hour timespan, she finally said yes. I have the dream team now, with her and Sosie always being at my side.

I finish up my set and wave to the crowd before being rushed off the stage during the commercial break. I was fortunate to be the last performer before the ball drops, so after the commercial, Aly and I will help start the countdown on live television.

"Mr. McNeer, you have thirty seconds before you need to stand at your mark," one of the producers tells me. I nod at them and go over to get Aly.

"Oh my God, it's *so* cold!" she says against my lips while I kiss her. I've got her wrapped in my arms, and I start to rub my hands up and down her back to warm her up. "Can we go back to the hotel now?"

"Not yet, darlin'. We get to help with the countdown." I grab her gloved hand and start pulling her to where we need to stand.

"Wait, I don't need to be on live television!" She tries to pull her hand out of my grasp, but I just hold on tighter.

"Baby, this is our first New Year's together, and not many people get to celebrate it in Times Square! You are not depriving me of my New Year's kiss," I tell her while throwing my arm around her shoulders to help lead her where the cameras are. I introduce her to Seth Ryan, the famous television personality who is hosting the live event. We stand on our marks and watch as the cameraman counts down with his fingers and points to us when we're live.

"I'm Seth Ryan, and you're watching the Rock N' Roll New Year's Eve Countdown. We're about ready to drop that ball, and Gavin

McNeer with his girlfriend, Alyson, are going to help me bring in the New Year!" Seth turns to look at me and winks. "Gavin, any famous last words you have for 2019?"

I grab the microphone from him with one hand and take the ring that has been hidden in my pocket with my other. "Why yes, Seth, I do have some famous last words." I get down on one knee in front of Aly, who looks like a beautiful shocked deer caught in headlights, and hold out the ring to her.

"Alyson Dawson, would you do me the honor of starting out 2020 as my fiancée?" Tears spring to her eyes, love radiating from them as she looks from the ring back up to me. "You're my entire world, Aly, and it doesn't exist without you. What do you say, darlin'? Will you be mine forever?" We are down to the last ten seconds of 2019 and the crowd starts going wild with chanting.

"Oh my gosh, are you kidding me?" she screams as she looks from me to the crowd and back to me. "A thousand times yes!"

I stand up and take off her glove to put the three-carat emerald-cut diamond on her finger. She barely even glances at the ring before throwing herself into my arms and crushing her lips to mine. I feel congratulatory pats on my back from Seth and some of the other guests, but I tune them out, my focus only on my future bride and starting this year off with a boom.

Epilogue 2

ALY

8 months later

I STAND IN my normal position on the side of the stage, watching my man strut his sexy self back and forth to the delight of the crowd. It's been three months since we got married, and it feels like we went from the wedding straight to touring the country festivals with his friend, Patty Douglas. It was a last-minute invite, one Gavin really couldn't afford to pass up, but nevertheless, we are grateful for this opportunity.

Gavin's new album just came out last month

from his new record label, and it's smoking up the charts. Not only that, but he has a couple songs he co-wrote with other artists being played all over the radio. This tour is our honeymoon, and being newlyweds on the road isn't as glamorous as it seems, but I've never been happier. I'm fulfilling my dreams of finding a man who loves me, working in the music industry with him, and traveling. I didn't think life could get any better.

But life is full of surprises, and lucky for us, those surprises all seem to be good ones.

The song ends to the roar of the crowd and Gavin's guitar player, Neil, looks over at me. I nod at him, a mischievous smile playing on my lips. Gavin is always doing crazy, outrageous, surprise gestures of love for me, and now I have one to give him in return.

"What's up, Chicago?" Neil screams into the microphone, and Gavin gives him a funny look, noting that Neil is going rogue. "Are you having a good time?"

The crowd goes wild as the house lights go on for us to see all of them.

"We want to thank everyone for coming out and seeing us tonight. Now, normally, I let

Gavin do all the talking during his show, but I had a feeling he was going to keep something very important to himself tonight."

Gavin starts to laugh at Neil, knowing full well what Neil's referring to.

"It's this sexy beast's birthday today!"

The crowd starts to cheer, and Sosie and I grab the shot trays I ordered. We walk on stage for the guys to drink a celebratory shot. We hand them out until they're gone and stay on stage to celebrate with the band.

"You sneaky little minx," Gavin whispers in my ear before kissing me hard on the lips. I hand him his shot, and the band with thousands of people in the crowd start to sing "Happy Birthday." We toast to Gavin after the song is done, but I stay on stage, with one more surprise up my sleeve.

"Gavin's wife, Aly, has a present for him that she wanted him to open on stage. She thinks it might help him perform a little better for you guys," Neil jokes, causing the crowd to cheer louder.

I take the thin, long box out of my pocket and hand it to Gavin, who looks at it confused. "Darlin', I don't need any presents from you, and this really looks too small to be a new microphone."

My heart starts pounding in my chest as he takes off the bow and rips off the paper. I suddenly feel queasy, wondering if this is even a good idea, because he might not like the gift.

He opens up the lid of the box, his smile fading as he stares at the positive pregnancy test. He looks up from it, his gaze starting at my belly before meeting my eyes. I breathe a sigh of relief when I see tears of joy spring to his eyes.

"You're not messing with me, right?" He gently embraces me and whispers in my ear, "I'm really going to be a daddy?"

I laugh and grasp the sides of his face. "You're going to be the best daddy in the whole universe."

"I fucking love you, Alyson McNeer." He kisses me hard, his tongue demanding entrance into my parted lips, not caring we are in front of thousands of people. I kiss him back with heat and desperation, a silent promise of more to come later.

He breaks our kiss but still holds me in his arms as he brings the microphone to his lips.

"This woman is the best gift I could've asked for, and tonight, she just gave me the second-best gift of my life. We're going to have a baby!" He grabs my hand and swings my arm up in the air, the crowd going wild.

Sosie and the band come over to embrace us, and Gavin gives me one more kiss before I walk off the stage for him to continue his show. As I watch the love of my life sing songs he wrote for me, I realize my life is now complete, and I can't wait for our next new adventure together.

Acknowledgements for Aurora Rose Reynolds

First, I have to give thanks to God, because without him, none of this would be possible. Second, I want to thank my husband. I love you now and always—thank you for believing in me, even when I don't always believe in myself. To my beautiful son, you bring such joy into my life, and I'm so honored to be your mom.

To every blog and reader, thank you for taking the time to read and share my books. There will never be enough ink in the world to acknowledge you all, but I will forever be grateful to each and every one of you.

I started this writing journey after I fell in love with reading, like thousands of authors before me. I wanted to give people a place to escape where the stories were funny, sweet, hot, and left you feeling good. I have loved sharing my stories with you all, and love that I've helped people escape the real world, even for a moment.

I started writing for me and will continue writing for you.

XOXO, Aurora

Acknowledgements for Jessica Marin

When I wrote *Until Valerie* for Aurora Rose Reynolds's Happily Ever Alpha World, I had no intentions of writing another novel about her sister, Aly. Then one day, someone in the Happily Ever Alpha World Facebook group asked about it, and more people chimed in and said they wanted it too. I was so happy people not only loved *Until Valerie*, but also wanted more by reading about Aly and Gavin's love story. Aurora took note of it and asked if I wanted to write it together. Um, hell yeah, I did, and we did it!! I truly hope you fell in love with Aly and Gavin as we did. If it weren't for those readers saying they wanted their story, this book probably wouldn't have happened. So, thank you!

Thank you to all of the readers and bloggers who take the time out of your day to read my work and support me. Your positive feedback and love mean the world to me.

Thank you to my friends and family, especially my husband and children. Without their support, I wouldn't be able to continue living my dream.

Thank you to my Misfits for your continued love, support, and promotion of all things Jessica Marin.

Please make sure you follow me on my social media pages and sign up for my newsletter at authorjessicamarin.com to be up to date with upcoming releases and book signings.

I look forward to our next adventure together!

About Aurora Rose Reynolds

Aurora Rose Reynolds is a *New York Times* and *USA Today* bestselling author whose wildly popular series include Until, Until Him, Until Her, Fluke My Life, Underground Kings, How to Catch an Alpha, and Shooting Stars.

Her writing career started in an attempt to get the outrageously alpha men who resided in her head to leave her alone and has blossomed into an opportunity to share her stories with readers all over the world.

To keep up to date on what's happening, join the Alpha Mailing List by subscribing at her website at www.aurorarosereynolds.com.

Signed paperbacks can be ordered off of Aurora's website at www.aurorarosereynolds.com.

About Jessica Marin

Jessica Marin began her love affair with books at a young age from the encouragement of her Grandma Shirley. She has always dreamed of being an author and finally made her dreams of writing happily-ever-after stories a reality. She currently resides in Tennessee with her husband, children, and fur babies. When she's not hanging out with her family, she loves watching a good movie, going dancing with the ladies, sniffing essential oils, and daydreaming of warm beaches, and world peace.

Jessica would love for you to join her on all of her available social media outlets.

About Boom Factory Publishing

Aurora Rose Reynolds and her husband, Sedaka Reynolds, created Boom Factory Publishing to use their experiences to expand and promote upcoming and existing indie authors.

With over six years in the industry, and millions of books sold worldwide, we know what it takes to become a successful author and we will use this knowledge to take our authors to the next level.

"As a successful hybrid author in this ever evolving industry, I know that you're only as successful as the team that is promoting you!" – Aurora Rose Reynolds

Please check out Boom Factory Publishing's website to see all of our talented authors and the books they have published.

boomfactorypublishing.com